The Boy Allies at Jutland

By

Robert L. Drake

The Boy Allies at Jutland

CHAPTER I

H.M.S. "QUEEN MARY"

A great, long, gray shape moved swiftly through the waters of the Thames. Smoke, pouring from three different points in the middle of this great shape, ascended, straight in the air some distance, then, caught by the wind, drifted westward.

It was growing dark. Several hours before, this ocean greyhound—one of Great Britain's monster sea-fighters—had up-anchored and left her dock—where she had been undergoing slight repairs—heading eastward down the river.

Men lined the rails of the monster ship. These were her crew—or some of her crew, to be exact—for the others were engaged in duties that prevented them from waving to the crowds that thronged the shore—as did the men on deck.

Sharp orders carried across the water to the ears of those on shore. The officers were issuing commands. Men left the rail and disappeared from the view of the spectators as they hurried to perform their duties. Came several sharp blasts of the vessel's siren; a moment later her speed increased and as she slid easily through the waters of the river, a cheer went up from both shores.

The crowd strained its eyes. Far down the river now the giant battleship was disappearing from the sight of the men and women who lined the banks. In vain, a few moments later, did many eyes try to pierce the darkness. The battleship was lost to sight.

The vessel that had thus passed down the Thames was H. M. S. Queen Mary, one of the most formidable of England's sea fighters. It was with such ships as the Queen Mary, supported by smaller and less powerful craft, that Great Britain, for almost two years of the great war, had maintained her supremacy of the seas.

This great ship was new in service, having been completed only a few years before the outbreak of the war. She was constructed at a cost of $10,000,000. She was 720 feet long, of 27,000 tons burden and had a complement of almost 1,000 men. For fighting purposes she was equipped with all that was modern.

In her forward turret she carried a battery of six 16-inch guns. Aft, the turret was similarly equipped. Also the Queen Mary mounted other big guns and rapid firers. She was equipped with an even half-dozen 12-inch torpedo tubes. She was one of the biggest ships of war that roved the seas.

The Queen Mary was one of the fleet of battleships that had patrolled the North Sea since the outbreak of hostilities. Already she had seen her share of fighting, for she had led more than one attack upon the enemy when the Germans had mustered up courage enough to leave the safety of the great fortress of Heligoland, where the main German high sea fleet was quartered.

It had been in a skirmish with one of these venturesome enemy vessels that the Queen Mary had received injuries that necessitated her going into dry dock for a few days, while she was given an overhauling and her wounds healed. True enough, she had sent the foe to the bottom; but with a last dying shot, the Germans had put a shell aboard the Queen Mary.

Her damage repaired, the Queen Mary was now steaming to the open waters of the North Sea, where she would again take up patrol duty with the other vessels that comprised the British North Sea fleet, under command of Vice-Admiral Beatty, whose flagship, the Lion, had taken up the additional burden of patrolling the Queen Mary's territory while the latter was being overhauled.

Aboard the battleship, the British tars, who had become fretful at the delay, were happy at the thought of getting back into active service. While they had been given an opportunity to stretch their legs ashore, they, nevertheless, had been glad when the time to steam back into the open sea had come. Now, as the Queen Mary entered the mouth of the Thames and prepared' to leave the shores of Old England for the broad expanse of the North Sea, they sang, whistled and laughed gaily.

They were going back where they would get another chance at the enemy, should he again venture from his lair.

Forward, upon the upper deck, stood two young officers, who peered into the darkness ahead.

"To my mind," said one, "this beats a submarine. Just look about you. Consider the size of this battleship! Look at her armament! Think of the number of men aboard!"

"You may be right," returned the second officer, "but we have had some grand times beneath the sea. We have been to places and seen things that otherwise would have been impossible."

"True enough; but at the same time, when it came to a question of fight, we have had to slink about like a cat in the night, afraid to show ourselves to larger and heavier adversaries. Now, aboard the Queen Mary, that will be done away with. Now we are the cat rather than the mouse."

"It may be that I shall come to your way of thinking in time," said the second speaker, "but at this moment I would rather have the familiar feel of a submarine beneath my heel. I would feel more at home there. Besides, we have lost one thing by being assigned to the Queen Mary that hits me rather hard."

"I know what you mean," said the first speaker. "We indeed have lost the companionship of a gallant commander. Captain Raleigh undoubtedly is a first class officer—otherwise he would not be in command of the Queen Mary—but we are bound to miss Lord Hastings."

"Indeed we are. Yet, as he told us, things cannot always be as we would like to have them. He was called for other service, as you know, and he did his best for us. That is why we find ourselves here as minor officers."

"Yes; and it's a whole lot different than being the second and third in command."

At that moment another young officer hurried by.

"Coming, Templeton? Coming, Chadwick?" he asked as he passed.

"Where?" demanded the two friends.

"Didn't you hear the call for mess?"

"No; By Jove! and I'm hungry, too," said the young officer addressed as Templeton. "Come along, Frank. We have been so busy talking here that we had forgotten all about the demands of the inner man."

The two hurried after the officer who had accosted them; and while they are attending to the wants of the inner man, as Templeton termed their appetites, we will take the time to explain how these two lads came to be aboard the giant battleship, steaming into the North Sea in search of the enemies of Great Britain and her allies.

Frank Chadwick was an American youth of some eighteen years. Separated from his father in Naples at the outbreak of the great war, he had been shanghaied aboard a sailing vessel when he had gone to the aid of a man apparently in distress. There he was made a prisoner.

Some days later he had been rescued by Jack Templeton, a young Englishman, who had boarded the vessel off the coast of Africa, seeking payment for goods he had sold to the mutinous crew. The two lads had been instrumental in helping Lord Hastings, a British nobleman, put through a coup that kept Italy out of the war on the side of Germany and Austria. Lord Hastings had become greatly attached to the lads, and when he had been put in command of a vessel, he had both boys assigned to his ship.

Through gallant service Frank and Jack had won their lieutenancies.

Later Lord Hastings had assumed command of a submarine and had made

Jack his first officer and Frank his second officer.

Through many a tight place the lads had gone safely, though they had faced death more than once, and faced it calmly and bravely. Also, at this period of the war, they had seen service in many seas. They had been engaged in the first battle of the North Sea, when Great Britain had struck her first hard blow; they had participated in the sinking of the German Atlantic squadron near the Falkland islands, off the coast of Argentina, in South America; they had fought in Turkish waters and in the Indian Ocean, and also had been with the British land forces when the Japanese allies of the English had won the last of the German possessions in China.

In stature and disposition the boys were as different as could be. Frank, though large for his age, looked small when alongside of Jack. The latter, though no older than his friend, was a huge bulk of a boy, standing well over six feet. He was built proportionately. Strong as an ox, he was, and cool of head.

Here he differed from Frank, who had something of a temper and was likely to do something foolish on the spur of the moment if he became angry. Jack had served as a damper for his friend's anger and enthusiasm more than once.

That they could fight, both boys had shown more than once. Jack, because of his huge bulk and great strength, was, of course, harder to beat in a hand-to-hand struggle than was Frank; but what the latter lacked in this kind of fighting, he more than made up in the use of revolver, rifle or sword.

Frank was a crack shot with a revolver; and more than once this accomplishment had stood them both in good stead. Each was a good linguist and conversed in French and German as well as in English. This also had been of help to them in several ticklish situations.

On their last venture, at which time they had been under command of Lord Hastings, they had reached the distant shores of Russia, where they had been of some assistance to the Czar. In reaching Petrograd it had been necessary for them to pass through the Kiel canal, which they had done safely in their submarine in spite of the German warships and harbor defenses. Also they had managed to sink several enemy vessels there.

Returning, Frank and Jack had gone home with Lord Hastings, where Lady Hastings had insisted that they remain quiet for some time. This they had done and had been glad of the rest.

One day Lord Hastings had come home with the announcement that he had been called back into the diplomatic service. It was the aim of the British government to align Greece and Roumania on the side of the Allies. Realizing that they could not hope to accompany Lord Hastings, and not wishing to remain idle longer, Frank and Jack had requested Lord Hastings to have them assigned on active duty at once. Lord Hastings promised to do his best.

And this was the reason that Frank Chadwick and Jack Templeton found themselves aboard H.M.S. Queen Mary when she steamed out to the North Sea on an evening in the last week of May, 1916.

CHAPTER II

A BIT OF HISTORY

Up to this time the German Sea fleet, as a unit, had suffered comparatively little damage in the great war. Sheltered as it was behind the great fortress of Heligoland, the British sea forces had been unable to reach it; nor would the Germans venture forth to give battle to the English, in spite of the bait that more than once had been placed just outside the mine fields that guarded the approach to the great German fortress itself.

To have attacked this fortress would have been foolhardy and the British knew it. The British fleet, powerful though it was, would have been no match for the great guns of the German fortress, even had the battleships been able to force a passage of the mine fields; and this latter feat would have been a wonderful one in itself, could it be accomplished.

Upon several occasions German battleships, cruisers and submarines had ventured from behind the mine field and had delivered raids upon the British coast, almost 400 miles away. How they escaped the eyes of the waiting British was a riddle that so far had not been explained. But while they reached alien shores in safety, they had not returned with the same success. Twice the British had come into contact with these German raiders and in each case the enemy had come off second best. Several German cruisers had been sent to the bottom.

After occasions like these, the Germans would lie long behind their snug walls before venturing forth into the open again. They held the British navy in too great awe to treat it lightly.

But the fact that the British were able to keep the German fleet bottled up was a victory in itself, though a bloodless one. Practically all commerce with Germany had been shut off. It settled down to a question of how long the German Empire could survive without the necessary food and other commodities reaching her shores. What little in the way of foodstuffs did reach Germany came by the way of the Scandinavian countries—Norway, Sweden and Denmark; also some grain was still being shipped in by the way of Roumania and was being transported up the Danube, which had been opened to traffic again after Serbia had been crushed.

But these supplies were not great enough to take care of the whole German population. In the conquest of Russian Poland, Germany had improved her lot somewhat, for the fertile fields had immediately been planted and a good crop had been reaped.

And the one thing that prevented Germany from importing the things that would in the end be necessary to her existence was the British supremacy of the sea, abetted now somewhat by the navies of France, Italy and Japan. German commerce had been cleared from the seven seas. What vessels of war had been scattered over the world at the outbreak of the war had either been sent to the bottom, captured or were interned in foreign ports. These latter were of no value to Germany.

It had been more than a year now since the last German commerce raider had been sunk. The German commercial flag was seen no more in the four corners of the globe. It appeared that Germany was nearing the end of her rope.

And yet, bottled up in Heligoland, remained the German high sea fleet practically intact. It was a formidable fleet and one, it seemed, that should not be afraid to venture from behind the protection of the fortress. And some day, the world knew, when all other ways had failed, this great fleet would steam forth to give battle to the British, in a last effort of the German Emperor to turn the tide in his favor; and while, in the allied nations at least, there was no doubt of the ultimate outcome of such a struggle, it was realized that the German fleet would give a good account of itself when it did venture forth.

Therefore, it was considered just as well that the British keep the German high sea fleet bottled up and give it no chance to reach the open, where, although the greater part might be sent to the bottom, some vessels might escape and embark upon a cruise of commerce warfare. This bloodless victory, it was pointed out, was of just as great value to Great Britain as if all the German ships of war had been at the bottom of the North Sea. Bottled up as they were, they were just as ineffective.

This was the situation, then, when the Queen Mary, with Jack and Frank aboard, steamed down the Thames and out into the North Sea to take up again her patrol of those waters; and there was nothing to warn those on board of the great battle that even now was impending and that was to result disastrously for Great Britain, even though the Germans were to suffer no less.

Mess over, Frank and Jack made their way to their own quarters amidships. Here they sat down and for some time talked over the events of the days gone by.

"I guess there will be nothing for us to do this night," said Frank at last. "We may as well turn in."

"I am afraid there will be nothing for us to do for some time to come," was Jack's reply. "I am afraid it will be rather monotonous sailing about the North Sea looking for German warships, when the latter are afraid to come out and fight."

"Well, you can't tell," said Frank. "However, that's one beauty of a submarine. You don't have to wait around for something to happen. You can go out and make it happen."

"That's so. But, by Jove! I wish these fellows would come out and fight! Maybe we could put an end to this war real quickly."

"Yes, but we might not," returned Frank.

"Why, don't you think we can thrash them?"

"I suppose we can; but at the same time they can do a lot of damage. Besides, some of them have come out. We've sunk some, of course, but the others have returned safely enough. I can't see any excuse for that."

"It does seem that they should have been caught," Jack agreed, "but I guess Admiral Jellicoe, Admiral Beatty and the admiralty know what is going on."

"Sometimes it doesn't look like it," declared Frank. "I suppose there are still some of these German submarines scooting about almost under our feet."

"I suppose so. However, ordinarily, as you know, they won't attack a battleship. It's too risky. If they miss with the first torpedo, the chances are they will be sunk."

"Well, we sunk a few," said Frank.

"I know we did; but we took long chances."

"The Germans take long chances, too."

"You must have a little German blood in you, Frank," said Jack, with a smile. "If I didn't know you better, I would think you were sticking up for them."

"No, I'm not sticking up for them; but they do things we seem to be afraid to do. To my way of thinking, we should have gone and cleaned up Heligoland a long time ago."

"By Jove! You want the enemy to win this war quickly, don't you?"

"No, but——"

"Come, now. You know very well what would have happened if we had tried to take a fleet into Heligoland. They would have blown us out of the water."

"Well, such things have been done," grumbled Frank. "I can tell you a couple of cases. At Mobile Bay——"

"Oh, I've heard all that before. But conditions now are absolutely different. What was done fifty years ago can't be done today."

"They aren't being done, that much is sure," replied Frank. "But this argument is not doing us any good. Me for a little sleep."

"I'm with you," said Jack.

And half an hour later, as the Queen Mary still steamed due east,

Frank and Jack slept.

Above, the third officer held the bridge. The great searchlight forward lighted the water for some distance ahead, and aft a second light cast its powerful rays first to port and then to starboard. There was not another vessel in sight.

Farther to the east, other British battleships patrolled the sea, their lights also flashing back and forth. It would be a bold enemy who would venture to run that blockade; and yet, in spite of this, the strictest watch was maintained. For the fact still remained fresh in the minds of the British that upon two occasions the Germans had run the British blockade; and both times the failure of the British to intercept them had resulted in heavy loss of life on the coast, where the German warships had shelled unfortified towns—against all rules of civilized warfare—killing thousands of helpless men, women and children.

It was against some such similar attack that the British warships were patrolling every mile of water. The British coast must be protected. No more German raiders must be allowed to slip through and bombard undefended coast towns.

Also, strict watch was kept aloft. For almost nightly now, huge German Zeppelins were sailing across the sea and dropping bombs upon the coast of Kent, upon Dover, and close even to London itself. It was feared that one of these monsters of the air might swoop down upon the battleships and, with a well directed bomb, send the vessel to the bottom of the sea.

All British war vessels were equipped with anti-aircraft guns and these were ever loaded and ready for action; for there was no telling what moment they might be called into use to repel a foe. Upon several occasions attacks of the Zeppelins had been beaten off with these guns, though, up to date, none had been brought down.

But now there had been perfected a new anti-aircraft gun. With this it was believed that the battleship stood a good chance of bringing down a Zeppelin should it venture near enough.

With such a gun the Queen Mary had been equipped as she was overhauled in dry dock. With this gun went four men. One to stand by the gun at night and keep watch of the sky and a second to do duty in the day time. The other two men stood relief watches and were of additional need should one of the first men be injured, taken sick or killed.

And so it was that, as the Queen Mary continued on her way, one of these men stood by his gun just aft of the bridge, watching the sky. Nor did he shirk his task.

Almost continuously his eye swept the dark heavens, following, as well as he could, in the path of one or the other of the searchlights. He used powerful night glasses for this purpose. Suddenly he gave a start. He looked closely again through his glasses. Then he uttered a cry of alarm.

The third officer, on the bridge, gave an exclamation.

"What do you see?" he demanded.

"Zeppelin," was the reply. "Douse the light aft. Have the man forward see if he can pick up the craft with his flash. About two points east by north."

There came sharp commands aboard the Queen Mary.

CHAPTER III

WARSHIP AND ZEPPELIN

A bell tinkled in the engine room of the Queen Mary. The ship slowed down. Captain Raleigh had been called by the third officer. He took the bridge and issued his orders sharply.

There was no telling whether the Zeppelin sighted by the man at the gun would attack the ship, but Captain Raleigh considered it best to be on the safe side. That was why he had left orders to be called immediately should an enemy appear.

Again a bell tinkled in the engine room, following an order from the commander of the Queen Mary.

The great engines stopped and became silent.

"Cut off all lights!" was the next command.

A moment later the great ship was in darkness.

Frank and Jack, in their quarters, were awakened by the sounds of confusion above. All hands had not been piped on deck, so most of the men still lay asleep, unconscious of what was going on above, but the two lads, dressing hurriedly, made their way on deck. They walked forward, toward the bridge.

All was dark and it was this that told Frank and Jack that something was going on.

"Wonder what's up?" said Frank.

"Airship, I guess," was the reply. "Can't see any other reason for extinguishing all lights."

Near the bridge the lads stopped and waited to see what would happen. All was quiet aboard. Not a sound came from the officers or the men on deck. Then Captain Raleigh commanded:

"Try the forward searchlight there. See if you can pick her up!"

The light flashed aloft; and there, so far above the Queen Mary as to be little more than a tiny speck, hovered a giant Zeppelin; and even as they looked, the airship came lower.

"She's sighted us," said Captain Raleigh to his first officer, who stood beside him. "Try a shot, Mr. Harrison."

The first officer passed the word and a second later there came the sound of the anti-aircraft gun. The gunner had taken his range at the moment the flashlight revealed the airship.

The shot brought no noticeable result.

"Fifteen knots ahead, Mr. Harrison!" ordered the captain.

He was afraid that the Zeppelin might drop a bomb on the ship; and from that moment until the end of the battle the Queen Mary did not pause. First she headed to port and then to starboard, manoeuvering rapidly that the German airmen might not be able to reach her with a bomb.

"Another shot!" commanded Captain Raleigh.

Still no result.

"Funny she doesn't rise and try and escape," said Frank.

"No, it's not," returned Jack. "They don't know anything about this new anti-aircraft gun. They believe they are out of range."

"Well, they're likely to hit us with one of those bombs, and then where will we be?" said Frank.

"If they hit us you won't know anything about it," was Jack's response.

Again the Queen Mary tried a shot at the Zeppelin.

A cheer went up from the members of the crew who stood upon deck; for the Zeppelin was seen to wabble.

"Nicked her," shouted the first officer.

Jack, standing near the rail, heard something whiz by his head. Instinctively the lad ducked. He knew in a moment what had passed him; he heard something splash into the sea.

"Bomb just missed us, sir!" he cried, stepping forward.

"Where?" demanded Captain Raleigh.

"Right here, forward, sir," replied Jack.

Captain Raleigh gave a quick command to his first officer, who passed it to the man at the wheel.

"Hard a-port!" he cried.

The ship veered crazily; and at the some moment, Frank, who was standing where Jack had been a moment before, heard something swish past.

"Another bomb, sir!" he reported.

There was no reply from the bridge. Captain Raleigh felt that, by bringing the ship's head hard to port, he had spoiled the range of the enemy in the air.

For some time no more bombs dropped near.

Again the Queen Mary fired at the Zeppelin; and again and again.

The last shot was rewarded by another cheer from the crew. The giant

Zeppelin was seen to drop suddenly.

The crew cheered loud and long for it appeared that the Zeppelin was about to drop into the sea. Down she came and still down; and then her descent suddenly halted.

To those aboard the Queen Mary this was unexplainable.

"Fire again, quickly!" shouted the captain.

The air gun boomed. At the same moment a man was seen to lean over the side of the Zeppelin. He dropped something.

Again Captain Raleigh acted promptly and brought the head of the Queen Mary around. The German bomb missed. Before another could be dropped, the man who manned the anti-aircraft gun fired again.

Another cheer from the crew.

The Zeppelin began to sink slowly.

"Full speed ahead!" cried Captain Raleigh. "They'll sink us!"

The Queen Mary leaped ahead just in time.

And then the Zeppelin dropped.

With a splash it hit the water perhaps a quarter of a mile from the British battleship. Came cries from the men, caught beneath the gas bag. At that moment Jack stood close to the bridge. Captain Raleigh saw him.

"Man a boat, Mr. Templeton," he called, "and rescue those fellows in the water."

Quickly Jack sprang to obey. Frank leaped after him. Hurriedly a small boat was gotten out and launched. A half dozen sailors sprang in and took up the oars. Frank and Jack leaped in after them.

The oars glistened in the glare of the searchlight as the men raised them and awaited the word.

"Give way," said Jack.

The boat sped over the smooth surface of the sea.

Close to the wreckage of the Zeppelin it approached; and cries told

Jack that some of the Germans still lived.

"Hurry!" he cried, and the men increased their stroke.

Near the wreckage Jack gave the command to cease rowing. A German swam toward the boat. Hands helped him in and he lay in the bottom panting. Other forms swam toward them. These, too, were lifted in the boat. And at last Jack counted fifteen Germans who had been saved.

"Are you all here?" he asked of a German officer.

"All but Commander Butz, sir," was the man's reply.

Jack commanded his men to row closer to the wreckage.

"Ahoy there!" he shouted, when he had come close.

The lad thought he heard a muffled answer, but he could not make sure.

He called again. This time the answer came plainer.

"Where are you?" asked Jack.

"Under the wreckage," was the reply.

Jack scrutinized the wreckage closely.

"Looks like it might sink any minute," he said "But we can't leave him there."

"What are you going to do?" asked Frank.

For answer Jack arose in the boat. Quickly he threw off his coat and kicked off his shoes. Then he poised himself on the edge of the boat.

"I'm going after him," he replied.

Before Frank could reply, he had dived head first into the sea.

With a cry of alarm, Frank also sprang to his feet and divested himself of his coat and shoes.

"Stay close, men!" he commanded. "I'll lend a hand if it's needed."

He, too, leaped into the water.

Rapidly, Jack swam close to the wreckage. He continued to call to the

German, and while he received an answer each time, he could not locate

the man. Twice he swam around all that remained of the huge Zeppelin.

By this time Frank had come up with him.

"Can't you find him?" he asked.

"No," returned Jack, "and I am rather afraid to swim under there. The balloon may sink and carry me under. But if I were certain in exactly what spot the man is imprisoned, I'd have a try at it."

Frank listened attentively; and directly the German's voice came again.

To Frank it seemed that the voice came from directly ahead of him.

"Lay hold of this end here," he said to Jack. "If you can lift it a bit

I'll go under and have a look."

"Better let me do it, Frank," said Jack.

"No; you're stronger than I am. You can hold this up better."

Jack did as his chum requested and a moment later Frank disappeared under the wreckage, diving first to make sure that he got under.

Under the water the lad swam forward. His hand touched something that was threshing about.

He felt sure it was the German. He rose. His head came in contact with something, but the lad opened his eyes and saw that he was above the surface. The imprisoned German was close beside him.

"Dive!" said Frank. "You can come out all right."

"Can't," was the reply. "My arm is caught."

Frank made a quick examination.

"I can loosen it," he said at last, "but I'll probably break the arm."

"Loosen it," said the German, quietly.

Frank took a firm hold on the arm at the elbow and gave a quick wrench. He felt something give, and when he released his hold on the man's arm, the latter sank suddenly.

Frank dived after him quickly. It was even as the lad feared. The German had fainted from the pain of the arm, which Frank had broken cleanly as he released it.

Frank dived deep and his outstretched hand encountered the German. The lad grasped the man firmly by the collar and then struck upwards. A moment later he succeeded in making his way to where Jack still tugged at the balloon.

Jack lent a hand and they dragged the German from beneath the wreckage. Then they towed him to the boat and other hands lifted him in. Frank and Jack clambered aboard.

"Give way!" said Jack, sharply.

The boat moved toward the battleship; and even as it did so, the mass of wreckage suddenly disappeared from sight with a loud noise.

Jack shuddered.

"Pretty close, Frank," he said quietly. "You can see what would have happened if you had still been under there."

CHAPTER IV

ATHLETICS

"Can you fight?"

The speaker was a young British midshipman. Jack and Frank stood at the rail, gazing off toward the distant horizon, when the young man approached them. The lads turned quickly.

"Can you fight?" demanded the young man again. His eyes rested on Jack.

"Well," said the latter with a smile, "I can if I'm pushed to it. Who wants to lick me now?"

The young midshipman also smiled.

"It's not that kind of a fight I'm talking about," he said. "You're new aboard, so I'll explain."

"Do," said Jack.

"Well, there has been considerable rivalry between the men of our ship and the crew of the Indefatigable. We had an athletic contest last year and they beat us, carrying everything but the standing broad jump. This year we are better fortified and we hope to get even. Among other things there will be a boxing match. Jackson, that's the man we had entered in that event, is ill. I have been elected to find a substitute. I sized you up as being able to hold your own with most."

"Well, if that's the way of it, you can count me in, of course," said

Jack. "When does this come off?"

"As soon as we come up with the Indefatigable. Probably tomorrow."

"What other events are there?" asked Frank.

"Plenty," was the reply. "Besides the boxing match and standing broad jump are the running broad jump; high jumping, a match with foils and a revolver contest."

"And are your lists filled?" asked Frank.

"I believe so. Why?"

"Well, I'd like to get in the revolver contest," replied the lad. "I'm pretty handy with a gun."

"I'll see what can be done," returned the midshipman. "By the way, my name is Lawrence."

They shook hands and walked off.

"Well, that's something to liven things up a bit," said Frank.

"Yes; but I didn't know they were doing such things in time of war."

"Neither did I; but it seems they are."

It was late that evening when Lawrence again approached the two lads.

"You're in luck," he said to Frank. "We are still one man shy on our revolver team. I have named you for the place."

"Thanks," said Frank. "I'll promise to do the best I can. By the way, where is this match to take place?"

"Right here. Last year it was pulled off on the Indefatigable."

It was drawing toward night when the Queen Mary, steaming swiftly, sighted smoke upon the horizon. Two hours later she slowed down a short distance from three other vessels, which proved to be the Indefatigable, the Invincible and the Lion, the latter the flagship of Vice-Admiral Beatty.

The commanders exchanged salutations; and among other things made arrangements for the athletic contest that was to take place aboard the Queen Mary the following day. This was explained to the men.

The day's events were to begin at nine o'clock. They were to come in this order: Standing broad jump, running broad jump, high jump, foil match, revolver contest and boxing match.

"You're last on the card, Jack," said Frank, with a laugh, when they were informed of the manner in which the events were to be pulled off.

"Hope I'm last on my feet, too," said Jack, with a laugh.

"Oh, I'm not worrying about you. You'll come through with flying colors. I hope I am not nervous, though."

"You won't be," said Jack, positively. "I know you and that revolver of yours too well."

"Guess we had better turn in early so as to be fit," said Frank.

And they did, retiring several hours after mess.

Every man aboard the Queen Mary was astir bright and early the following morning. Each man was filled with enthusiasm and each was ready to wager his next year's pay on the outcome of each event. But there was to be no gambling. Admiral Beatty had issued orders to that effect.

At eight o'clock the championship entrants from the Indefatigable came aboard, accompanied by many of their companions, who would be present to cheer them on. Officers as well as men were greatly interested in the day's sports. Admiral Beatty could not be present, but Captain Reynolds, of the Indefatigable, stood by Captain Raleigh, of the Queen Mary, as the first event was called.

"We're going to get even with you this time, Reynolds," said Captain

Raleigh.

"Oh, no you won't. The score will be two in our favor after today."

They became silent as four men, two from each ship, made ready for the standing broad jump.

The jumping was superb. After eight attempts one man from each ship was eliminated; and at length the Indefatigable man won.

"Two points for us, Raleigh," said Captain Reynolds, jotting down something on the back of an envelope.

"Don't crow, we'll get you yet, Reynolds," was Captain Raleigh's reply.

The running broad jump was won by the Queen Mary's entrants. Then it was Captain Raleigh's time to smile.

"Told you so," he said to Captain Reynolds.

"Oh, you won one event last year," was the reply. "This high jump comes to us."

And it did. The score was now four to two in favor of the Indefatigable. Then came the match with foils and this also went to the Indefatigable, making the score nine to two, for this match carried five points for the winner. Also, the pistol contest and the boxing match carried five points each.

"We've got you now, Raleigh," laughed Captain Reynolds. "Nine to two. You've got to take both of the next two events to win. It can't be done."

"It has been done," was the reply.

"It won't be this time," was the reply. "I think we will win the revolver contest, for I have some pretty fair shots, but if we don't, we are sure to take the boxing match. We've a surprise for you there. Here they go."

The revolver match was on. There were three men on each team. The first mark was set, a target at twenty yards with a six-inch bull's eye. Frank fired first. He hit the bull's eye easily. So did the others, all except one of the Indefatigable crew, who was thus eliminated, much to his disgust, as the spectators jeered him.

The next shot at a smaller mark eliminated one of the Queen Mary's crew. An Indefatigable man and a Queen Mary man both missed the next mark and there remained but Frank for the Queen Mary and a man named Simpson for the Indefatigable.

The target had been removed to sixty yards and the bull's eye was but two inches. Frank fired and scored a hit. So did Simpson. Next both hit the mark ten yards farther back.

A one-inch bull's eye was substituted. Frank fired first. He scored a clean hit. Simpson also hit the eye, though not so squarely. Still it counted a hit.

Now the bull's eye was reduced to half an inch, and at seventy yards it seemed almost impossible to hit it. This time Simpson was to fire first. Carefully he took deliberate aim and fired.

A shout went up from the Queen Mary men who stood near.

"Missed it by a hair," said one. "Beat it, Chadwick! Beat it!"

"He can't beat it! Hooray! We've won!" This from the Indefatigable's crew.

"Good shooting, old man," said Frank, quietly, as he took his position.

Carefully he measured the distance with his eye.

Then he raised his revolver slowly, and seeming scarcely to take aim, fired.

And a yell went up from the Queen Mary's crew.

"Bull's eye! Bull's eye!" they cried, and danced and capered about the deck.

Frank had won. He had hit the bull's eye squarely.

The men rushed up and danced about him.

"Good work!" they cried. "Five points for us. Nine to seven now. We'll win this yet!"

Simpson approached Frank and extended a hand.

"Good shooting, son," he exclaimed.

Simpson was a man well along in years, and he put this touch of familiarity to his words to make Frank realize that they were sincere. "I used to be something of a shot myself," he said. "But I guess you are better than I ever was."

Frank took Simpson's hand.

"You would probably beat me next time," he said.

Simpson shook his head.

"Not in a thousand years," he said, and walked off.

Meantime, Captain Raleigh and Captain Reynolds were having it out.

"Told you so! Told you so!" exclaimed the former, as pleased as a boy.

"We'll beat you yet, sure."

"No, you won't, Raleigh," said Reynolds, with a wink. "I'll tell you something. Ever hear of a man named Harris?"

"Yes; I know several men by that name."

"Ever hear of Tim Harris?"

"By George! You mean Tim Harris, of the Queen Elizabeth?"

"The same."

"The champion of the British fleet, eh? You mean to tell me you have rung him in on us?"

"We didn't ring him in," was the reply. "He was transferred to the Indefatigable before the Queen Elizabeth went to the Dardanelles. We've been saving this up as a little surprise."

Captain Raleigh had lost his look of optimism.

"Then our man should be warned," he said. "He may wish to withdraw."

"It is only fair to tell him who his opponent is," agreed Captain

Reynolds. "I guess we should have done it long ago."

"I'll tell him," said Captain Raleigh.

At this moment there was a loud cheer from the crew of the Queen

Mary.

"Here he comes!" they shouted.

Jack, stripped to the waist and wearing a pair of trunks, had appeared on deck. Two men accompanied him. These, it seemed, were to be his seconds. Jack caught sight of Frank and smiled.

And again the crew of the Queen Mary went wild.

CHAPTER V

THE FIGHT

The champion of the Indefatigable had not yet appeared on deck; and the crew of the Queen Mary strained their necks hunting him out.

"Bring out your champion!" they called. "What's the matter with him? Is he afraid?"

The men of the Indefatigable returned these compliments with jeers of their own.

"Oh, just wait!" they howled.

Captain Raleigh, in the meantime, had approached Jack and his seconds.

"It is only fair to warn you," he said quietly, "that the man whom you are to oppose is Tim Harris, champion of the British fleet."

Jack was surprised.

"I didn't know that, sir. I thought he was with the Queen Elizabeth."

"Well, he's here; but I didn't know it until a moment ago. It will be no dishonor to you if you wish to withdraw. A man must be in perfect trim to stand before Harris."

"Why," said Jack, in surprise, "I can hardly do that now, sir. The men are depending on me."

Captain Raleigh smiled frankly.

"You are all right, boy," he said. "At your first words I thought you were afraid. But you cannot hope for victory."

"I always hope for victory, sir, and I shall do my best. I am no novice."

"Perhaps not; but Harris is almost a professional; in fact, I may say, a good deal better than many professionals. He is fast for a man of his size and has a terrible right-hand punch. I have seen him box often. If you are decided to go on with this, a word of warning. Watch that right hand of his like you would a hawk."

"I shall remember, sir," replied Jack. "Thank you."

"All right then," said Captain Raleigh. "I like your spunk. Good luck to you."

Captain Raleigh walked back to Captain Reynold's side.

"Will he withdraw?" asked the latter.

"He will not. He says the men are depending on him and he must go through with it."

"By Jove! a fine spirit!" exclaimed Captain Reynolds. "I hope he is not too easily disposed of."

"I don't think he will be," said Captain Raleigh, quietly. "Someway, I have a feeling that you haven't carried off the honors yet."

"But it's foolish to talk like that, Raleigh," said Captain Reynolds.

"You know this man, Harris."

"I suppose it is foolish, but it's the way I feel just the same. Ah!

There's Harris now."

Tim Harris had appeared on deck; and the crew of the Indefatigable went wild. Now for the first time the crew of the Queen Mary knew who Jack's opponent would be; and after a look at Harris, they became strangely silent. Then one voice called:

"Never mind who he is. Templeton can lick him, anyhow!"

The others took up the cry and Jack smiled.

Now the referee called the principals to him and gave them their instructions.

"No hitting in clinches, and clean breaks," he said.

Jack and Harris nodded that they understood. As the two stood there together, the crowd sized them up.

Jack, standing well above six feet, still was not as tall as his opponent, who topped him by a full inch. Their arms were about of a length, but Harris was big through the chest and his arms seemed more powerful than Jack's. A close observer, however, would have seen that while Jack was in perfect physical condition, Harris carried a trifle too much fat—not much, but still a trifle. With the battle anywhere near equal, this fat might prove to Jack's advantage.

Jack's arms showed strength, but the muscles were not knotted like those of Harris. Harris was perhaps twenty-eight years old, Jack almost ten years younger. Jack had the youth, but Harris had the experience of many hard encounters. It appeared that the odds were heavily against Jack.

Jack and Harris sized each other carefully. Jack smiled. So did Harris.

As they touched gloves, Harris said:

"You're a nice boy. I don't want to hurt you too much, so I'll make this short"—the referee had announced that the match was to be for ten rounds.

"Don't worry about me," said Jack. "I can take care of myself. If the match is short you won't find me on the deck."

Harris would have replied, but at that moment the referee called:

"Time!"

Jack leaped lightly backward even as Harris aimed a vicious blow at his head, apparently trying to make good his word to end the battle at once. The blow missed Jack's face by the fraction of an inch. Harris followed up this blow with a right and left, which Jack blocked neatly, and then brought his right up, trying to upper cut.

Jack leaped backward and the blow grazed his chin. Before Harris could recover, Jack stepped quickly forward and planted a sharp right and a hard left to Harris' nose. Harris stepped back and wiped away a stream of red.

It was first blood for Jack and the crew of the Queen Mary sent up a wild cheer.

But Harris only smiled. He was not to be caught so easily again.

These two blows had given the Indefatigable champion some respect for

Jack's ability. He advanced more carefully this time. He feinted

rapidly and shot his left forward, quickly followed by his right. But

Jack had not been deceived and caught both blows upon his forearms.

"You're all right, boy," said Harris, admiringly, "It's a pleasure to box with you."

"And I may say the same," said Jack.

They fell to it again.

As Harris stepped quickly forward his foot slipped and he fell to one knee.

"Hit him when he gets up!" came a cry from the crowd.

Instead, Jack lowered his guard and extended a hand. He helped his opponent to his feet. Then he stepped back and the battle continued.

Now Jack decided that he would feel the other out. He feinted rapidly, once, twice, and struck out with a right; and he staggered back suddenly, for something had suddenly come up under his chin with terrible force. In a moment Jack realized what it was. It was Harris' right, which Captain Raleigh had warned him against. Had the blow been timed perfectly, Jack realized, the fight would have been over then and there.

Guarding desperately, Jack managed to fall into a clinch, where he hung on until his head cleared. As he stepped back the referee called time. The first round was Harris' by the margin of that hard uppercut.

"I'll be a little more careful of that right," Jack confided to his seconds, as he again advanced into the ring.

Again the lad assumed the offensive, keeping careful eye on his opponent's right fist. Again Harris tried to reach Jack's chin, but this time Jack blocked the blow. He knew he would not be caught that way again. Jack feinted three times, twice with his left and once with his right, and then the right crashed against Harris' ear. The man staggered back and before he could recover Jack planted two hard blows —right and left—to his sore nose. Desperately, Harris rushed into a clinch.

Again the crew of the Queen Mary cheered.

"And what do you think of that, eh?" asked Captain Raleigh of Captain

Reynolds.

"The boy is a fighter," was the latter's reply. "But wait; experience will tell."

Harris became more cautious. He circled around Jack, lightly, dancing about on his toes. The lad followed him quietly. Suddenly, Harris' left fist shot out. Jack blocked, but before he could recover, Harris launched himself like a catapult and a series of right and lefts descended on Jack's face, neck, ears and abdomen.

Jack staggered back and Harris followed him closely, giving him no rest

Jack was still retreating at the bell.

Again in the third and in the fourth round Jack seemed to be getting the worst of it. In the fifth he braced and sent in as good as he received. In the sixth he almost floored Harris with a straight right to the side of the jaw; and in the seventh Harris was kept on the defensive.

But in the eighth Jack again encountered Harris' right and the force of the blow sent him reeling. All through the round Harris followed up this advantage, and at the bell, it seemed that Jack would be unable to continue the fight.

But his head cleared in the one minute rest period; and he fought through the ninth round carefully. The lad realized now that, so far, Harris had the better of the encounter and that, if he hoped to win, it must be by a knockout. So, while Harris was trying in vain to put in a finishing punch, Jack husbanded his strength, determined to make a strong effort in the final round.

The rest refreshed him still more; and as time was called for the tenth, Jack cast discretion to the winds and leaped forward.

In spite of this, he was cool, however, and kept his eye peeled for the movement that would tell him Harris was about to launch his right.

A right and left he landed to Harris' sore nose. Then Harris rushed. Jack was forced back around the ring by the force of this rush and backed against the ropes; but he bounded out with great force and landed a vicious left to the side of Harris' jaw. Then they clinched.

As the referee parted them, Jack saw the movement for which he had been watching. Harris again was about to launch that terrible right. The lad waited calmly.

"Swish!"

It flashed forth faster than the eye could see. But it had not come too quick for Jack, who was expecting it.

The blow was aimed for the point of the chin and would have ended the fight right there. But, judging the distance exactly, Jack moved his head a trifle to one side; and Harris' fist flashed by his chin by the fraction of an inch.

With all his force behind the blow, Jack put a straight left to Harris' jaw. A terrible jolt to the abdomen followed; and, as Harris head came forward again, Jack pivoted on his heel and struck with his right.

He had judged the time and the distance perfectly. His right fist caught Harris squarely upon the point of the chin. There was a "smack" that could be heard even above the cheering of the Queen Mary's crew, followed by a crash as Harris fell to the deck. With half a minute of the last round to go, Jack had knocked the man out and won the day for the Queen Mary by a score of twelve to nine.

And the crew cheered again!

CHAPTER VI

SCOUTING

Harris remained prostrate on the deck.

Quickly, Jack pulled off his gloves and, leaning down, he picked up the unconscious man and carried him to his own cabin. There he bathed the man's face and brought him back to consciousness.

"How do you feel, old man?" he asked.

Harris looked at the lad queerly.

"So you beat me, eh?" he said. "Well, to tell you the truth, after the fifth round I expected it. I am no match for you and I know it. Do you realize that you are the champion of the British fleet now?"

"I hadn't thought of that," was Jack's reply.

"You have defeated the champion, so your title is undisputed," said

Harris.

He rose from the bunk where Jack had placed him and felt tenderly of his chin.

"Quite a wallop," he said calmly. "Well, let me congratulate you. I am glad that, as long as I had to be defeated some day, it was you who turned the trick."

He extended a hand and Jack grasped it heartily.

"You would probably down me next time," he said.

"Not a chance," replied Harris. "I know when I have met my superior."

He moved toward the door. There he paused for a moment and said:

"Well, I must go and dress now. I hope that I may see you again before long."

"I am sure I hope so, too," returned Jack.

Hardly had Harris taken his departure when running feet approached Jack's cabin. A moment later a crowd of sailors burst into the room. Before Jack realized what was going on, they had seized him, hoisted him to their shoulders and rushed out on deck again. There, for perhaps half an hour, they paraded up and down, cheering wildly.

They lowered him to the deck, however, when Captain Raleigh and Captain

Reynolds approached. The former spoke first.

"I must congratulate you upon your remarkable exhibition," he said.

"You are a brave boy."

Jack flushed and hung his head.

"When I am mistaken I admit it," said Captain Reynolds. "You are more than a match for Harris at any time."

"I did the best I could," said Jack, sheepishly.

"Well, it was pretty good," said Captain Reynolds.

With Captain Raleigh he moved away.

Frank now approached and accompanied Jack back to their cabin, where

Jack got info his uniform.

"Some scrapper, you are," said Frank. "I thought you were done for once or twice, though."

"I thought so myself," returned Jack, with a grin. "I was pretty lucky in that last round, if you ask me."

"Harris was pretty unlucky, I know that," said Frank, grimly. "Hurry up, it's time to eat."

Jack's fight was the talk of the day aboard the Queen Mary; and aboard the Indefatigable, too, for that matter. In fact, all the British fleet within wireless radius knew before night that there was a new champion of the British fleet; and they cheered him, though he could not hear.

It was upon the following morning, while the Queen Mary steamed about in the North Sea, that Jack and Frank embarked upon their first piece of work since they had been assigned to the giant battleship.

Both lads were in their cabin studying, when an orderly announced that Captain Raleigh desired their presence. They obeyed the summons at once.

"And how do you feel today?" asked Captain Raleigh, as he eyed Jack, quietly.

"First rate, sir."

"Feel like another fight?"

"No, sir. I don't make a practice of that sort of thing."

"I'm glad to hear that. How would you like to take a little trip?"

"First rate, sir. Where to, sir?"

"Well, that's rather a difficult question," returned Captain Raleigh.

"Here, read this," and he passed the lad a slip of paper.

Jack did as commanded. This is what he read:

"Large number of enemy aircraft reported flying over North Sea, fifty miles south of you, every night. Investigate.

(Signed) "BEATTY."

Jack passed the slip of paper back.

"Well?" exclaimed Captain Raleigh.

"Yes, sir," replied Jack. "You want me to find out what's going on, sir?"

"Exactly. Can you run a hydroplane?"

"No, sir; but Frank here can."

"Who?"

"Lieutenant Chadwick, sir."

"Oh," said the commander, "so he is Frank, eh? All right. Then here is what I want you two to do. Take the hydroplane aft and fly south. Take your time and see what you can find out. The matter may amount to nothing, and then again it may forebode something serious."

"Very well, sir," replied Frank. "When shall we start, sir?"

"You may as well start immediately. It is hardly possible, judging by the tone of that message, that you will find anything by daylight, but at least you can be on the ground by night."

"Very well, sir," said Jack, and waited to see if there were any further instructions.

Captain Raleigh dismissed the two lads with a wave of his hand.

"That is all," he said. "Report the moment you are able to do so."

The two lads saluted and returned to their own cabin.

"You see," said Frank, "we didn't have to wait very long to find something to do."

"I see we didn't," agreed Frank. "Now, the first thing to do is shed these uniforms."

"What for?"

"So that we shall not be taken for British should we fall among the enemy. We'll put on plain khaki suits."

"Well, whatever you say," said Frank.

This was the work of but a few moments; and half an hour later the two lads soared into the air in one of the Queen Mary's large hydroplanes.

"This is something like it, if you ask me," said Frank, as he bent over the wheel.

"Pretty fine," Jack agreed, raising his voice to make himself heard above the whir of the propellers and the noise of the engine. "I wouldn't mind flying all the time."

"Where do we want to come down, Jack?" asked Frank.

"Let's see. The message said the enemy was flying about fifty miles south. They probably won't be out before dark, so I should say it might be well to go a little beyond that point."

"All right. But we may miss them in the darkness tonight."

"By Jove! That's so! Funny I didn't think of that. Let me think a moment."

"No use of thinking," said Frank, "I have a scheme that will work all right."

"What is it?"

"Why, we'll stop right in the path taken by the enemy planes and then drop down upon the water."

"So the Germans can see us as they fly by, eh?"

"They won't see us in the dark," said Frank. "We'll be a pretty small spot down on the water. They will be looking for nothing so small."

"I guess you are right, after all," Jack agreed. "At least it's worth trying. We'll be sure to hear them flying above; and if we went beyond the lane of travel, or didn't go far enough, we might not even see them."

"Exactly," said Frank. "Well, there is no hurry, so I may as well slow down a bit."

He did so and they went along more leisurely.

"Can't see what the Germans would be flying about here for," said Jack, "and I have been trying to figure it out ever since I read that message."

"So have I," declared Frank, "If they were Zeppelins I could understand it; they would be going and returning from raids on the British coast; but surely they would not venture that distance with aeroplanes."

"I wouldn't think so. Still, you never can tell about those fellows.

They do a lot of strange things."

"So they do. Say!" Frank was struck with a sudden thought. "You don't suppose the presence of many of those fellows heralds the advance of the German fleet, do you? They might be just reconnoitering, you know."

"No, I hardly think that could be it. The Germans are afraid to venture out. They know they'll get licked if they do."

"Well, those aeroplanes come out every night for some purpose, that's sure," said Frank. "It's a wonder to me the Germans haven't tried to sneak out in great force before now. They could come along here without any trouble, or they could make the effort farther north, say near Jutland."

"Well, I suppose they'll try it some day," said Jack, "but not right away. How much farther do we have to go?"

Frank glanced at his chart and then at his speedometer.

"About fifteen miles," was his reply; "and then we'll be there too soon."

The lad was right. It was not three o'clock when the hydroplane came to the spot the lads had selected to descend.

"Well, here we are," said Frank.

"Guess we may as well go down, then," said Jack. "Some of those fellows are likely to be prowling about and spot us."

"Just as you say," agreed Frank.

He set the planes and the machine glided to the water, where it came to rest lightly.

"Glad there is no sun," said Jack, "it would be awfully hot down here."

And there the lads spent the afternoon. Darkness came at last, and with its coming, the lads made ready for whatever might occur. Eight o'clock came and there had been no sounds of airships flying above. The lads strained their ears, listening for the slightest sound.

And, shortly after nine o'clock, their efforts were rewarded. Jack suddenly took Frank by the arm.

"Listen!" he exclaimed in a low voice.

CHAPTER VII

AMONG THE ENEMY

To Frank's ears came a distant whirring. To ears less keen than the lad's the sound, which came from above, might have been some bird of the night flapping its wings as it soared overhead. But to Frank and Jack both it meant something entirely different. It was the sound for which they had been waiting. It was an airship.

Through his night glass Jack scanned the clouds and at last he picked up the object for which he sought. Almost directly overhead at that moment, but flying rapidly westward, was a single aeroplane. So high in the air was the machine that it looked a mere speck and Jack was unable to determine from that distance whether it was British or German.

"See it, Jack?" asked Frank in a low voice.

"Yes," was the reply. "A single craft, perhaps half a mile up."

"No more in sight, eh?"

"Not yet. This one is heading west."

"Guess we had better get up that way, then," said Frank.

Jack assented.

A moment later the hydroplane was skimming swiftly over the water. For perhaps three hundred yards Frank kept the craft on the water; then sent it soaring into the air above.

There was not a word between the two boys until the hydroplane was a quarter of a mile in the air. Then Jack said:

"Make your elevation half a mile and then head west, slowly. The chances are there will be more of them. In the darkness we can let them overtake us and mingle with them in safety."

Frank gave his endorsement to this plan and the machine continued to rise. At the proper elevation, Frank turned the hydroplane's head westward and reduced the speed to less than thirty miles an hour. So slow was its gait, in fact, that it had the appearance of almost standing still.

Jack scanned the eastern horizon with his glass.

"See anything?" asked Frank.

"Thought I did," was the reply, "but whatever I saw has disappeared now. Guess I must have been mistaken."

But Jack had not been mistaken.

Far back, even now, a fleet of perhaps a dozen German air planes were speeding westward. For the most part they were small craft, having a capacity of not more than three men, with the single exception of one machine, which, larger than the rest, carried four men. The air planes were strung out for considerable distance, no two being closer than two hundred yards together.

And in this manner they overtook the hydroplane driven by Frank and

Jack.

Jack, again surveying the horizon with his night glass, gave an exclamation.

"Here they come, Frank," he said. "Let her out a little more."

Frank obeyed without question and the speed of the hydroplane increased from something more than thirty miles an hour to almost sixty. And still the Germans gained.

"This will do," said Jack, leaning close to Frank. "They'll overtake us, but believing we are of their number, there is little likelihood that they will investigate us very closely. We can fall in line without trouble and accompany them wherever they go."

"Suits me," said Frank. "Just keep me posted on their proximity."

Gradually the Germans reduced the distance and at length the first plane was only a few yards behind the craft in which Frank and Jack were risking their lives. The German craft flashed by a moment later without paying any attention to the hydroplane.

"Little more speed, Frank," called Jack.

The hydroplane skimmed through the air faster than before and the next German craft did not overtake it so easily; but at length it passed, as did a third and a fourth.

"Here's a good place for us to fall in line," Jack instructed.

Again Frank increased the speed of the hydroplane and it moved swiftly in the wake of the fourth German craft. After that no enemy air plane passed them.

"Any idea where we are?" asked Frank of his chum.

"We're not far off the Belgian coast, but how far west I can't say," returned Jack. "Don't suppose it makes any particular difference, though."

"I guess not."

Frank became silent and gave his undivided attention to keeping the

German plane ahead of him in sight.

And in this manner they proceeded for perhaps another half hour.

Then the machine ahead of Frank veered sharply to the south. Frank brought the head of his own craft in the same direction and the flight continued.

"Headed for the Belgian or French coast, apparently," said Jack to himself. "Wonder what the idea is?"

Now the craft ahead of that in which the two boys rode reduced its speed abruptly. Frank cut down the gait of his own craft and they continued on their way more slowly.

"Nearing our destination, wherever that is," muttered Jack.

The lad felt of his revolvers to make sure that they were ready in case of an emergency.

"Land ahead," said Frank, suddenly.

Jack gazed straight before him. There, what appeared to be many miles away, though in reality it was but a few, was a dark blur below. Occasionally what appeared to be little stars twinkled there. Jack knew they were the lights of some town.

"Guess that's where we are headed for, all right," he told himself.

Behind the British hydroplane the other German airships came rapidly, keeping some distance apart, however. Jack leaned close to Frank.

"Just do as the ones ahead of you do," he said quietly. "I don't know where we are nor what is likely to happen. Keep your nerve and we'll be all right."

"Don't worry about me," responded Frank. "I'm having the time of my life."

Jack smiled to himself, for he knew that Frank was telling the truth. There was nothing the lad liked better than to be engaged in a dangerous piece of work and more than once his fondness for excitement had almost ended disastrously.

"Frank's all right if he can just keep his head," muttered Jack. "I'm likely to have to hold him in check a bit, though."

They had approached the shore close enough now to perceive that the distant lights betokened a large town.

"Probably Ostend," Jack told himself, "though why they should come this way is too deep for me."

But Jack was wrong, as he learned a short time later.

The town that they now were approaching was the French port of Calais and it was still held by the French despite determined efforts of the Germans at one time or another to extend their lines that far. The capture of Calais by the Germans would have been a severe blow to England, for with the French seaport in their possession, the Germans, with their great guns, would have been able to command the English channel and a considerable portion of the North Sea coast.

When it appeared that the German aircraft would fly directly over the city, the leading machine suddenly swerved to the east. The others followed suit.

The night was very dark, and in spite of the occasional searchlight that was flashed into the air by the French in Calais, the Teuton machines so far had been undiscovered. Now, hanging low over the land, a sudden bombardment broke out from the German air planes.

It was not the sound of bombs that came to the lads' ears; rather the sharp "crack! crack!" of revolver firing. Jack and Frank gazed about them quickly, for they believed, for the moment, that the Germans had encountered a squadron of French airships.

But there was no other machine in sight save the German craft.

"What in the world is the meaning of this?" Frank asked of Jack.

"Don't know," returned the lad, "but I guess I'd better join in."

He drew his revolver and fired several shots in the air.

"Seems to be expected of us," he said. "We don't want to disappoint them."

The German aircraft now headed straight for the city of Calais. Frank sent his machine speeding in the same direction. Then, just as it appeared they would fly directly above the city, the first German craft began to descend. The others did likewise and a moment or so later they all came to earth in the center of what Frank and Jack could see was a small army camp; and as they alighted from their machines, the lads saw that it was an Allied camp and not a German.

"Must be Calais," said Frank to Jack in a whisper. "Have we been mistaken? Are these French and British machines?"

"Well, it looks like it," returned Jack. "We'll keep quiet and let the other fellows do the talking."

A French officer now approached the pilot of the first aircraft.

"We heard the firing aloft a moment ago," he said. "Did you encounter the enemy?"

"We were pursued all the way from the German lines," was the reply.

"Anyone hit?"

"I think not, though I believe we accounted for one or two of the enemy."

"Good. Will you fly again tonight?"

"Yes; but not before midnight."

The French officer withdrew.

At this one of the aviators raised a hand and the others gathered about him, Frank and Jack with them. All wore khaki clothing and their features were concealed by heavy goggles.

"Careful," whispered the aviator. "A false move and we are discovered.

Spread out now and see what you can learn. Gather here at midnight."

He waved a hand and the Germans, for such Jack and Frank now knew them to be, separated. When the two lads were alone a moment later, Jack said:

"Well, this is what I call a piece of nervy business. What shall we do?

Inform the French commander immediately?"

"No. I have a better plan that that. They can hardly work any mischief tonight. What information they learn will avail them naught for we can warn the French commander later. We must find out what they are up to. We'll stick close and follow them back to the German lines, if necessary."

"Good, then! Guess we had better do a little skirmishing about. It will keep suspicion from us should we be watched."

"All right," said Frank. "Come on."

CHAPTER VIII

A STARTLING DISCOVERY

With the coming of midnight Frank and Jack returned to the spot where the aeroplanes had been parked. Several of the German aviators already had returned. The man who appeared to be the leader announced that they would await the arrival of the others before taking to the air.

The others arrived one at a time until all were present but two. The machines were in readiness to ascend the moment the missing men arrived. The aviators were at their posts.

Suddenly there came a shout. A moment later the two German aviators who were delaying the departure burst into sight at a dead run.

"Quick!" called one. "We are discovered!"

Immediately the others—Frank and Jack among them—leaped into their machines and soared into the air. The last comers also leaped for their craft and succeeded in getting above ground just as rifles began to crack in the French camp.

Came a sudden cry from the machine nearest that of Frank and Jack. The lads saw a man rise to his feet, throw up his arms and pitch, head foremost, toward the ground. The aircraft, freed of a guiding hand, rocked a moment crazily and then turned over, hurling its other occupant into space.

There was a cry of anger from aboard some of the other German craft, but no man raised a hand to stay the flight of his car. It would have been suicide and the Germans realized it. They sped away into the darkness whence they had come. Frank and Jack, in their British hydroplane, went with them.

For an hour or two the aeroplanes sped through the darkness at undiminished speed; then the foremost craft slowed down. The others did likewise.

"Surely we haven't reached the German lines already?" said Jack. Frank shrugged his shoulders.

"You know about as much of what is going on as I do," he returned.

"Evidently we are going down, however."

The lad was right.

The leading German plane swooped toward the earth and the others followed its example. A few minutes later all had reached the ground safely and their occupants had alighted.

The two lads glanced around. It was very dark. A short distance to the north they could see the broad expanse of the North Sea, stretching away in the night. The dark waves lapped the shore gently with a faint thrashing sound. The water was very calm.

Except for the figures that had alighted upon the shore in the darkness there was not a human being in sight. To the south, to the east and west stretched miles and miles of sand dunes. Just these sand dunes and the waters of the North Sea—there was nothing else in sight.

At a signal the men gathered around the man who appeared to be the leader. Frank and Jack thanked their lucky stars that the night was very dark, for otherwise they would have been in imminent danger of being discovered; and each lad realized that it would go hard with them should their true identities be penetrated.

The darkness served them like a shield. Nevertheless, both lads kept their hands on their revolvers. Each had determined that if discovered, he would make an effort to escape in the nearest of the aircraft. Each knew that there was little hope of such an escape, but, realizing what was in store for them should they be discovered and captured, they had decided it would be better to die fighting than to be stood up against a wall and shot, or, possibly, hanged.

The group of men on the bench became silent as the leader addressed them.

"Men," he said, "it is to be regretted that we have discovered so soon. There was still work to be done before the hour for our great effort to crush the British fleet. However, to a certain extent we have been successful. We have managed to sow the seed of suspicion in the minds of our enemies. Prisoners, whom we have allowed to be taken, have let slip words that will lead the British to think our fleet will slip from its base and approach England from the south. We know better than that. We know that on the night of May 31—which is tomorrow—our fleet will strike the British off Jutland."

There was a subdued cheer from the assembled Germans. The speaker continued:

"Through our efforts the British fleet has been scattered. The main portion of the fleet lies to the south and will be unable to reach Jutland in time to save the portion of the British fleet there from destruction. Of course, should wind of the move reach the British there would still be time for the fleet to gather. But no such word will reach the enemy. After sinking the first section of the British fleet, our vessels will steam south and meet the main British fleet. The numbers will be nearer equal then. We shall be victorious."

Again there was a subdued cheer, in which Frank and Jack joined for the sake of appearances. Again the speaker continued:

"I shall now explain the reason we have landed here. Our part in the work has been done. Here we shall remain until nightfall tomorrow. We shall then sail north and take part in the battle. In my pocket here," he tapped the breast of his coat, "are instructions I shall read to you before we leave. Until that time we shall rest here, for we have done work enough for the present. We shall be safe here. Our position now is directly between two French lines and for that reason we shall not be disturbed. Of course, if it becomes necessary, we can take to our machines and get out of harm's way. We have provisions and water enough to last us; and while the weather is warm, it is still cool enough. At any rate, we shall have to make the best of it."

The man ceased speaking and beckoned the others to follow him. He walked a hundred yards to the east. There he made a mark in the sand with his foot.

"Until the time for us to move has come," he said, "let no man set foot beyond that line. I make this rule for safety's sake."

He walked two hundred yards from the sea itself and repeated the operation and instructions; and then to the west.

"Within these bounds," he said, "we will spend tonight and tomorrow. The man who disobeys these instructions shall be shot. Do I make myself plain?"

There was a murmur of assent.

"Very well," said the leader. "Now you are all left to your own devices. First, however, I shall pick the watches for the night."

Frank and Jack, at this, slunk well back into the crowd, for they did not wish to be scrutinized closely. But they need have had no fear. The leader of the Germans laid a hand on the shoulders of the two men nearest him.

"You two," he said, "shall stand guard the remainder of the night, one to the southeast and one to the southwest. But do not venture beyond the boundaries I have laid down."

The Germans saluted and moved away.

The leader moved toward the sea and none of the others followed him. Instead, some walked a short distance to the east, others to the south and still others to the west. They threw themselves down in the sand. A few remained near the airships.

Frank and Jack walked a short distance toward the sea, but kept some distance behind the German leader, who stood looking off across the water, apparently deep in thought. The lads sat down upon the ground.

"Well," said Frank, "what are we going to do about it?"

"Do!" echoed Jack. "Why, there is only one thing we can do—one thing we must do! We must get away from here and warn the fleet!"

"All right," said Frank, "it sounds easy; but how?"

"Well, that doesn't make any difference. We've got to do it."

"And the moment we have gone our absence will be discovered, the Germans will know the fleet has been warned and the attack will be given up," said Frank. "And we don't want anything like that to happen. It will be the first time the Germans have mustered up courage enough to come out and give battle. We don't want to frighten them off."

"We don't want to let them sneak up on a part of our fleet unguarded, either," declared Jack.

"Of course not. You say we must give the warning. We'll try, of course. But first, why not let's put all the aeroplanes except the one we want out of commission?"

"By Jove! a good plan! We'll do it."

"Exactly," said Frank. "Then there is still another thing."

"What is that?"

"Why, we want the instructions that fellow carries," and Frank waved a hand in the direction of the German leader. "He was kind enough to let us know he has them. We'll have to take them away from him."

"Say!" exclaimed Jack, "you've laid out quite a job for us, haven't you?"

"It's got to be done," declared Frank.

"Well, all right, but we shall have to be careful."

"Right you are," Frank agreed, "one little slip and the whole thing will be spoiled."

"Then there must be no slip," said Jack, quietly

"I agree with you there. Now the question arise? as how the thing may best be done."

"We'll have to wait until they're all asleep," said Jack.

"You forget the sentinels won't sleep," said Frank.

"No, I don't; and they will be the first disposed of. They are not looking for enemies from within, you know. You walk up to one and I'll walk up to the other. We'll be challenged when we get close, of course. Then it will be up to us to silence those fellows before they can make an outcry."

"We'll try it. Then what?"

"Then we'll come back and put the airships out of commission as carefully as possible."

"That's easy enough. All we have to do is to let out the 'gas.'"

"Next we'll have to go through the commander's pockets without arousing him."

"That's more difficult, but I suppose it can be done."

"Next we'll have to get our hydroplane to the water. Fortunately, we came down closer to the sea than the others. We should be able to do that without awakening the sleepers."

"Then," said Frank, "we climb in and say goodbye, eh?"

"That's it."

"All right. We'll work it that way then. It's as good as any other. Now we'll keep quiet until we are sure everyone is asleep."

Their plans thus arranged, the lads became quiet. They said not a word as they waited for sleep to overcome the Germans, but gazed out quietly over the dark sea.

CHAPTER IX

THE PLAN WORKS—ALMOST

"Time to get busy."

It was Frank who spoke. All was quiet among the sand dunes. The commander of the Germans had laid down upon the ground, some distance from the others, half an hour before. Snores from various points announced that most of the men were sleeping soundly.

Jack and Frank got to their feet

"Careful," said Jack as they separated. "Remember, don't give your man a chance to let out a cry."

Frank nodded in the darkness and walked slowly toward the sentinel he had selected to silence. Jack moved in the other direction.

As Jack came within a few yards of his prey, the man raised his rifle and commanded:

"Halt!"

"It's all right," said Jack. "I couldn't sleep and it was lonesome back there. I want company."

The German lowered his rifle.

"It's lonesome here, too," he said. "Wish you had been selected for my job."

"I wouldn't have minded it tonight," said Jack, approaching closer.

The German reached in his pocket and produced a pack of cigarettes. He extended the pack to Jack.

"Have one?" he invited.

Jack accepted a cigarette.

The German produced a match. He laid his rifle upon the ground as he struck the match upon the leg of his trousers.

It was the moment for which Jack had been waiting.

Quickly his revolver leaped out. In almost the same instant he reversed it and before the German realized what was about to happen he brought the butt down on the man's head with great force.

The man fell to the ground without a sound.

Frank, advancing upon the other German, also was challenged when he drew close, but he, too, engaged his prey in conversation. As the man turned his head for a moment to gaze across the dark sand, the lad struck him violently over the head with his revolver butt. The German dropped like a log.

A few moments later Frank and Jack met again near the first aeroplane.

"It'll have to be quick work here," Jack warned "We haven't a whole lot of time, you know."

Frank nodded that he understood. Rapidly they passed from one plane to another letting out the gasoline. Five minutes later, with the exception of their hydroplane, which rested some distance away, every craft upon the beach was dry. They were absolutely useless—or so the lads thought.

"Now for the papers," said Jack, as he straightened up after tinkering with the last machine.

Cautiously the two lads advanced upon the sleeping German. Frank raised his revolver and would have brought it down on the man's head had not Jack stayed him with a gesture.

"No need of that," he said. "I don't like to hurt a man except when it is absolutely necessary."

Frank put the revolver back in his pocket.

Gently, Jack thrust his hand into the German's pocket. He fumbled about a moment and then drew forth a paper. Turning his head aside he struck a match and glanced at the paper. Then he nodded his satisfaction.

"This is it," he said.

Frank, at that moment, had risen to his feet. Believing the work was accomplished, he was moving off toward the hydroplane. As Jack now made to get to his feet, he chanced to glance at the German he had just relieved of the papers.

The lad uttered an exclamation of surprise, and no wonder. The man's eyes were open and gazed straight at Jack. In his hand he held a revolver and it was levelled at Jack's head.

"Hands up!" said the German, quietly.

There was nothing for Jack to do but obey or be shot. His hands went high in the air, but he still retained the valuable papers.

"Drop those papers," was the next command.

Jack obeyed and the papers fluttered to his feet. The German reached out and picked them up with his left hand while with his right he still covered the lad with his revolver.

"So you're a spy, eh?" said the German.

Jack made no reply, but a gleam of hope lighted up his eye; for, Frank, chancing to turn for some unexplainable reason, had taken in the situation and was now advancing on tiptoe to his friend's aid.

"How did you get here?" demanded the German, making ready to rise.

Again Jack made no reply; but none was necessary, for at that moment Frank had come within striking distance. His arm rose and fell, and as his revolver butt descended upon the German's head, the latter toppled over in a heap.

Quickly, Jack stooped and again recovered the papers he had taken so much pains to get.

"Come on!" cried Frank. "We haven't time to fool around here. The rest of this crowd is likely to wake up in a minute or two."

Jack followed his friend across the sand. They laid hold of the hydroplane and rolled it toward the water. In it went with a splash and Frank cried:

"Climb aboard quickly!"

Jack needed no urging and a moment later the two boys were ready for flight. And then, suddenly, there was the crack of a revolver behind them and a bullet flew close to Jack's ear.

The German leader had recovered consciousness, and springing to his feet, dashed to the water's edge and fired point blank at the machine.

Fortunately, in his excitement his aim was poor and he missed. Before he could fire again, Frank wheeled about and his revolver spoke sharply.

The German threw up his arms, and with a gasp, pitched headlong into the sea.

But the sounds of the two shots had aroused the sleeping camp. Wild cries came from the shore, followed by heavy footfalls as the Germans rushed toward the water.

"Hurry, Frank!" cried Jack.

As lightly as a fairy the hydroplane skimmed over the water; then went soaring in the air. Frank gave a loud cheer.

"Safe!" he exclaimed.

But the lad was wrong.

From on shore came a chorus of angry cries and imprecations. Hastily the Germans made a rush for their aeroplanes to give chase. None would move. Followed more cries and angry shouts.

"Wait," said one German. "I've some gasoline."

Rapidly he opened up a big can, which he took from the bottom of his machine. Quickly the tank was filled and the man climbed into the pilot's seat. Another jumped in with him.

"Give us some of that gasoline!" cried another.

The German shook his head.

"Not enough," he replied. "We'll overtake those fellows and then come back for the rest of you."

The aeroplane leaped skyward and started in pursuit of Frank and Jack.

The two boys, believing that they were safe, were going along only at a fair rate of speed when Jack's keen ears caught the sound of the pursuing machine.

"They're after us, Frank!" he called.

"Impossible!" replied Frank. "How can they fly without gas?"

"Well, they're coming, all the same," declared Jack.

He produced his two revolvers and examined them carefully.

"You run this thing and I'll do what fighting is necessary," he said. "Wish I could shoot like you can; but I can't; and I can't run this machine either."

The German aeroplane was gaining steadily.

"He can outrun us," said Frank, quietly. "There is only one, thank goodness. You'll have to bring him down, Jack."

"I'll try," was Jack's reply. "If I had a rifle I might be able to pick him off now."

"Well, he won't hardly have any the best of it," said Frank. "The chances are he has no rifle either."

Frank was correct in this surmise.

Rapidly the German aircraft gained.

"Crack!" the German had fired the first shot.

It went wild. Jack fired, but with no better result.

"Hit anything?" asked Frank, without turning his head.

"No," said Jack, "but neither did the other fellow."

"Try it again," said Frank.

Jack did so; but again the bullet went wild. All this time the two craft were flying straight out to sea.

Once more the German fired and Jack felt something whizz overhead.

"This is getting too close," the lad muttered to himself. Then he called to Frank.

"Slow down, quick!"

Frank had no means of telling what plan Jack had in mind, but he did not hesitate. The hydroplane slowed down with a jerk.

The pilot of the German craft was caught off his guard. He dashed upon the hydroplane. But as he neared it he swerved to the left to avoid a collision. It was what Jack had expected. Standing up in his precarious position, Jack took a snap shot at the pilot as the German craft swept by.

At that close distance, in spite of the rate of speed at which the enemy was travelling, a miss was practically impossible.

The German machine swayed crazily from one side to the other; then dived.

"I got him, Frank!" shouted Jack.

Both lads gazed over the side at the falling enemy.

Suddenly the machine righted and descended more slowly.

"By Jove! a cool customer," said Frank. "He's regained control of the plane. He'll be up again in a moment."

Again they watched the foe carefully.

"No, he won't," said Jack, "he's still going down."

"Then we may as well be moving," said Frank.

"Hold on!" shouted Jack. "We can't leave those fellows there. They may get to shore or be picked up. Then they would give the warning and all our efforts would be for naught."

"Right," said Frank. "We'll go down after them."

The hydroplane descended slowly.

CHAPTER X

THE FIGHT ON THE WATER

Below, the fallen aeroplane rested upon the surface of the sea. In the darkness, it was hard for the lads to tell just how badly the craft was damaged and whether it would float; but Jack's idea was to be on the safe side.

While still some distance from the water, there was a shot from below.

"Hello!" said Jack. "They're alive and kicking, all right. Wonder if we can't go down and get them from the water."

"It's a better plan, I guess," said Frank. "We'll have an even break then. This way they have all the advantage."

He opened up the engine and the hydroplane ran some distance from the position of the men below. Then he shut off the motor and allowed the plane to glide down to the sea.

With the craft riding the swell of the waves, Jack picked up the enemy with his night glass. The disabled craft also was riding the waves gently perhaps five hundred yards away.

Jack gave the position to Frank, and the hydroplane approached the foe slowly. Within a range that would make accurate revolver shooting possible, the hydroplane came to a halt. As it did so there was the sound of a revolver shot from across the water and something whizzed overhead.

"Must have some pretty fair shooters over there," said Frank, quietly. "However, they can't see us any better than we can see them. Of course, they can see our craft all right, the same as we can see theirs, but they can't spot us."

"No; nor we can't spot them, which makes it worse," said Jack.

"We'll try a couple of shots for luck," said Frank.

He raised his revolver and fired quickly twice. His efforts were rewarded by a scream, apparently of pain.

"Must have hit one of them," he said grimly.

Again a revolver across the water flashed and the two lads heard a bullet whistle by.

Jack fired but without result and then Frank fired again.

There was another scream.

"Either got the other one, or the same one again," said Frank.

They waited some moments in silence, but no further shots came from the foe.

"By Jove!" said Jack, "you must have got them both. Let's go and have a look."

Slowly, Frank started the hydroplane and they bore down on the enemy.

Now they were two hundred, then one hundred yards away.

"Must have got them, all right," said Frank. "I——"

The flash of a revolver from the disabled craft interrupted him. It was closely followed by another and then two more.

With a sudden move, Frank changed the course of the hydroplane. He felt a sharp pain in his left shoulder.

"Got me," he called to Jack.

The latter was alarmed.

"Where?" he demanded.

"Left shoulder," said Frank, quietly. "Nothing serious, though."

Jack levelled his revolver and fired rapidly at the enemy. His pains were rewarded by howls of derision.

"They tricked us, all right," said Jack, as he reloaded.

"That's what they did. I should have known better, too. They almost settled us."

"We've got to get them, some way," declared Jack.

"Show me how, and I'll go along with you," declared Frank.

"Well, I've got a scheme, but I don't know whether it will work or not."

"Let's hear it."

"All right. But first, can you manage this plane all right with that bad shoulder?"

"Sure; it's not very bad."

"All right then. Well, you keep under cover about here, moving about just enough to spoil the aim of the foe. I'll drop over the side and swim to the enemy. I can get there unobserved, all right, because they won't be expecting me. I'll pull one of them over and settle with him first. Then I'll get the other."

"I don't know," Frank considered the plan. "I suppose it might work, but there is nothing sure about it."

"There's nothing sure about anything," declared Jack. "But it's better than staying here all the rest of the night. Besides, we must hurry, you know."

"That's right," agreed Frank. "All right, then. So be it. Will you take your gun?"

"No use," said Jack. "It would be wet by the time I got there. Here I go."

"Good luck," Frank called after him.

Gently, Jack lowered himself over the side of the hydroplane, first divesting himself of his coat and shoes; then struck out for the disabled aeroplane.

Slowly the lad swam, for he did not wish to betray his coming by the sound of a splash. The distance was not great and a powerful swimmer, such as Jack, could cover it easily in a few moments.

Jack did not approach the enemy craft from the front. Giving it a wide berth, he swam around it and then, turning quickly, bore down upon the aeroplane more swiftly. He swam with his head barely above the water, and he was ready to dive immediately should he be sighted.

There was not a sound aboard the aeroplane as Jack drew close to it.

Raising his head slightly, he could see no human form.

"Funny," the lad muttered to himself. "Wonder where they keep themselves. No wonder we couldn't hit them."

He was within a few feet of the disabled craft and he now rose higher in the water to get a good look about. Still he saw no one.

Twice around the machine the lad swam and not a human being did he see.

"There is something awfully queer about this," he told himself. "I'll go aboard."

He laid hands on the aeroplane and scrambled aboard. Quickly he sprang to his feet, ready to tackle any foe that might have seen him crawl aboard. Nothing happened.

Jack made a careful inspection of the disabled plane. Then, as he still gazed around, a sudden thought struck him. Without taking time to consider it, he sprang suddenly to the side of the plane and leaped into the water and with swift and powerful strokes struck out for his own craft.

Jack had hit upon the solution of the desertion of the German aeroplane.

Even as Jack had lowered himself from the hydroplane and swam across the water, the Germans in the other craft had done the same thing. Both sides had struck the same plan almost simultaneously. Jack, in making a wide detour as he approached the foes' machine, must have passed the two Germans in the water.

Now, realizing that the Germans must be close to the hydroplane, had they not already reached it, and remembering that Frank was wounded, Jack felt a sudden dread steal over him. His long, powerful strokes sent him through the water at great speed.

But the Germans had not made their presence known to Frank yet. Neither was as swift a swimmer as Jack, and for that reason, their progress through the water had been considerably slower. Also they had gone very cautiously.

A short distance from the hydroplane, one had swum to one side of the plane and the second to the other. The Germans also had discarded their revolvers, for they had realized they would be useless after their trip through the water. Also, not being expert swimmers, they had wanted to be unhampered by weight as much as possible.

Frank was still guiding the plane about occasionally to avoid a chance bullet from the enemy, but at the moment the Germans came close, he had stopped the craft and was peering into the darkness, straining his ears for the sound of a struggle that would tell him Jack was engaged with the enemy.

Suddenly a sound came to his ears from across the water, but it was not what he expected, although it was in Jack's voice:

"Frank! Look out! They are after you!"

Instantly, the lad understood the situation. He drew his revolver with his uninjured arm and sprang to one side of the aeroplane. As he did so, a figure reached up and grabbed him by the hand so that he could not fire. At the same time a second figure clambered aboard the craft from the opposite side. Frank raised a cry:

"Hurry, Jack!"

Jack needed no urging. He was swimming through the water as fast as possible.

With a sudden move, Frank jerked his hand loose from the grip that held him and turned just in time to encounter the second German. Frank raised his revolver and fired quickly; but the German ducked, and before Frank could fire again, he had come up close to Frank and grappled with him. In vain Frank sought to release his arm so that he could bring the weapon down on his opponent's head. The man clung tightly.

A sudden lurching of the hydroplane told Frank that the second German was coming aboard. Unmindful of his wounded shoulder, Frank struggled on. With a sharp kick of his right foot he succeeded in knocking the first German's legs from beneath him; and again the lad tried to raise his revolver to shoot the second German, who now advanced.

But the latter was too quick for him. Closing with the lad, the man knocked the revolver from the boy's hand with a quick blow. The weapon spun into the sea.

The first German returned to the attack.

"Get him quick!" he shouted. "There is another one around here some place."

Jack, at this moment, was within a few yards of the boat.

"You bet there is!" he said between his teeth. "And he'll be there in a minute."

He did not call encouragement to Frank, for he wished to get aboard the plane, if possible, before the men could stay him.

The two Germans rushed Frank simultaneously, and bore him back in the plane. At the same instant, Jack, unmindful of danger that might lurk aboard and thinking only of Frank's danger, laid hold of the plane and climbed aboard. Then he stood erect and shouted:

"Come on, you cowards! Here's the other one!"

CHAPTER XI

DAWN—AND A NEW ENEMY

The two Germans, just about to throw Frank overboard, turned quickly at the sound of this new voice. They wasted no time.

"At him!" cried one, and leaped.

The other sprang after him.

Jack, with his feet wide apart and arms extended, braced himself to receive the shock; and when it came he was ready. Frank, in the meantime, sank down in the plane almost unconscious, for one of the Germans had all but choked the life from him.

As the first German sprang, Jack met him with a straight right hand blow to the face and the man reeled back. The second, seeing the fate of his companion, dived for Jack's legs and seized them, pulling the lad down.

Jack felt out with his left hand and encircled the German's neck. Then he squeezed. The German gasped for breath as his wind was shut off. His hand searched his belt and presently flashed aloft with a knife. Jack saw it. Releasing his hold on the man's throat, he seized the knife arm with his left hand and twisted sharply, at the same time driving his right fist into the man's face.

There was a sharp snap and a cry of pain. The knife fell clattering to the deck of the plane. Jack, very angry, rose to his feet, stooped over, and picking up the German as though he had been a child, heaved him overboard.

"So much for you!" he muttered.

He stepped across the body of the second German to Frank's side and stooped over him. Gently he raised his chum's head to his knee.

Frank's eyelids flickered and directly he opened his eyes.

"How do you feel, old man?" asked Jack.

Frank struggled free from his chum's grip and sat up. He shook his head once or twice and then rose to his feet.

"I'll be all right in—Look out!" he broke off suddenly.

He dodged. But Jack, not realizing the import of Frank's words, remained still. He felt something hot sear the lobe of his ear. Wheeling abruptly, the lad saw the German whom he had first knocked unconscious facing him with levelled revolver—the weapon was Jack's own, which he had left behind when he swam to the enemy's aeroplane.

The German faced him with a smile.

"Hands up!" he commanded.

But Jack, with a few drops of blood trickling from his ear, suddenly became very angry. He objected to being shot at from behind.

"Put down that gun!" he commanded in a cold voice. "Put it down before

I kill you!"

The German was struck by the menace in the lad's tones, and for a moment he hesitated and the revolver wavered. Then he braced and brought the weapon up again.

But that moment of hesitation decided the issue. In spite of the fact that the revolver was pointed right at him, and that only a few feet away, Jack took a quick step forward.

The German fired. Jack swerved a trifle. The bullet plowed through the sleeve of his shirt and touched the skin; but that was all.

Again the man's hand tightened on the trigger, but he never fired again. Jack's powerful left hand seized his wrist and twisted the revolver from it Then, still grasping the wrist, the lad wheeled on his heel. The German left the spot where he had been standing as though pulled by a locomotive. He was lifted high in the air and, as Jack gave a jerk and then released his hold, the man went sailing through the air and dropped into the sea with a loud splash.

And at the same moment the intense darkness was shattered. The first faint streak of dawn showed in the east.

Jack sat down. Frank did likewise.

"That settles that," said Jack, briefly. "Now we had better get away from here. We haven't any too much time."

Frank, without a word, took his place at the wheel.

"Feel fit?" asked Jack.

Frank nodded, though he felt terribly faint.

"Sure you can make it?" Jack continued.

"Yes," replied Frank.

"Well, I just wanted to know," said Jack, "because here comes a German torpedo boat."

Frank was startled. He turned in his seat, and there, not a mile and a half away, was a ship of war. She was flying the German flag and was making directly for the spot where the British hydroplane rested.

"By George! Won't we ever get out of this?" the lad muttered.

"We won't unless you hurry," said Jack.

"But those two Germans. Won't they be picked up and give the alarm?"

"One of 'em won't," said Jack, grimly, "and I feel pretty safe about the other, too. Let's get up in the air."

Frank tinkered with the motor and took a firm grip on the wheel. But the hydroplane did not move.

"Something wrong," said Frank, quietly.

"What?" demanded Jack.

"Something wrong with the motor. It won't work."

Frank had bent over and was examining it carefully.

Came a shot from the German torpedo boat.

"If we don't get out of here pretty quick," said Jack, quietly, "we won't get out at all."

Frank made no reply, but continued to tinker with the engine.

A second shot from the German torpedo boat. It skimmed the water ahead of the hydroplane. Jack gazed toward the vessel. As he did so a small boat put off from the German and headed toward them.

"They're coming after us, Frank," said Jack, "a whole boatload of 'em.

How long will it take you to fix that thing?"

Frank uttered an exclamation of satisfaction.

"I've found it," he cried. "Five minutes," he answered Jack's question.

"Five minutes is liable to be too late," returned Jack, measuring the distance to the rapidly approaching German boat with his eye. "However, hurry as much as you can."

Frank did not take his eye from his engine.

"How far away?" he asked as he worked.

"Three quarters of a mile," replied Jack, calmly.

"Lots of time for us, then," said Frank, still working as swiftly as possible.

"Maybe," replied his chum. "Don't forget they carry pretty fair rifles with them."

"If we can get started before they shoot, I'll guarantee they don't get us," returned Frank.

"Well, they'll get us if you keep talking and don't get a move on there," said Jack. "They're coming like the wind."

"That's just the way I'm working. She's almost fixed row. Can you hold them off?"

"What, with a single revolver against a score of rifles? Not much.

They're right on us now. How's that engine?"

"Fixed!" cried Frank at that moment, straightening up.

"All right. Let her go then," said Jack, calmly. "They don't know yet that we're going to run. They have made no preparations to fire. Evidently they think we shall wait for them."

Even while Jack was speaking, the hydroplane began to move slowly over the surface of the water. Very slowly it went at first, then faster and faster.

"Halt!" came a cry from the German boat.

Jack picked up his cap and waved it at the Germans.

"Some other time," he called back. "We're terrible busy today.

Goodbye."

The German officer gave a sharp command. Several sailors sprang to their feet and blazed away at the hydroplane with their rifles. Bullets flew by on all sides, but none struck home.

Again Jack waved his cap.

"Very bad shooting," he remarked. "Looks like some of my—Hello! That wasn't so bad."

For the lad's cap, which he had been waving in derision at the pursuing foe, was suddenly carried from his hand by a German bullet.

"By Jove!" said Jack, quietly, "I wouldn't have lost that cap——" He gazed at it as it floated in the water.

And at that instant Frank sent the hydroplane soaring into the air with a lurch. Jack glanced down into the water.

"Hold on, Frank!" he cried.

In response to this command, Frank slowed down.

"What's the matter now?" he demanded.

"Why, one of our erstwhile German friends has come to life. He was just about to lay hold of us when you came up in the air. Great Scott! What do you think of that?"

"What do I think of what?"

"Why, the Germans in the boat have just shot him."

"Shot whom? The German?"

"Yes; they saw him coming after us and evidently thought he was a friend of ours. Poor fellow! To be shot down by one of his own countrymen. And so goes the last chance the Germans had of learning that we have discovered their plans."

"Then it is a good thing for us they shot him."

"For us, yes. But think of the irony of it!"

"Well," said Frank, "I wouldn't like to have shot him, defenseless as he was; and I didn't want you to. That's why I didn't suggest having a look for him before we came up."

"I couldn't have done it," returned Jack.

"No; nor I; and yet duty would have demanded it. For with him alive, there always remained a chance that he would give the warning."

"It just goes to show," said Jack, slowly, "that even fate sometimes works on the side of the right."

"True."

Unconsciously, Frank had allowed the speed of the hydroplane to diminish during this conversation, and the crew of the German boat again had found themselves within range. They had started to abandon the chase when the plane soared aloft, but when it had slowed down, they had resumed the pursuit, hoping that something had gone wrong with the craft.

Several bullets flew about the machine.

"Great Scott! They're at it again!" cried Jack. "Let's get away from here right now."

"All right, here she goes," said Frank. "Full speed ahead!"

CHAPTER XII

THE BOYS GIVE THE WARNING

One other adventure, it transpired, was to befall Frank and Jack before they found themselves once more aboard the British battleship, Queen Mary; and while it did not result seriously, both lads once more approached the very door of death.

The morning sun was well above the horizon when Jack, shading his eyes, made out in the distance a smudge of smoke.

"Smoke ahead, Frank," he called.

"Hope it's the Queen Mary" replied the lad. "It should be if I have calculated correctly."

A few moments later the outline of a large ship of war loomed up ahead.

"Can you make her out yet?" asked Jack.

"No; but she's built like the Queen Mary"

The hydroplane sped on.

"By Jove! She is the Queen Mary" cried Frank, a few moments later.

"We're in luck."

Frank was right. As the hydroplane drew nearer it was plain to make out that the vessel was the giant battleship the lads had quitted the day before.

"Wonder what Captain Raleigh will think of our information?" said

Frank, with a chuckle.

"Don't know. We've been pretty fortunate, though. I hope we are in time."

"So do I. The trouble is, our ships are scattered so far apart that they may not be able to assemble quick enough in sufficient strength to beat off the enemy."

"Don't worry; they won't get very far," said Jack, confidently.

"Oh, I know that. But if they should happen to come upon a small portion of our fleet we are likely to get the worst of it."

"Well, there is no reason why they should be able to do that now. We know their plans."

"That's true, too. And they won't, unless it is decided to engage them in spite of their numbers, trusting reinforcements will arrive in time."

And, though the lad had no idea he was making a prophecy, that is just what actually occurred.

The hydroplane now was less than a quarter of a mile from the Queen Mary and Frank reduced its speed abruptly. Whether this sudden slowing down had anything to do with what followed it is hard to tell; but, no sooner had Frank reduced the speed of the craft, than the plane wabbled crazily.

"Look out, Jack!" shouted Frank. "She's going down!"

Jack had not realized that there was anything wrong and now he did not grasp the full significance of Frank's words. What Jack thought Frank meant was that he was going to glide down to the deck of the battleship. Frank, however, knew that there was something seriously wrong with the craft. His first thought had been to jump after crying out to Jack, but seeing that his friend had not understood, Frank stuck to his post, trying as well as he knew how to bring the plane to the sea as gently as possible.

For a moment it seemed that he would succeed, for, as it neared the water, the plane righted itself. Frank drew a breath of relief. But his relief was short-lived.

After remaining upon a level keel for one single instant, the hydroplane turned turtle.

There came a cry of warning from aboard the Queen Mary, and even before the falling boys struck water, boats were lowered over the side, manned, and dashed to the rescue.

Although Frank had been unable to maintain the plane on an even keel, his efforts had done some good; for the distance was not so great from the water when the plane capsized as it would have been but for his strenuous efforts.

Jack uttered a cry of alarm as he felt himself being hurled into space, for he had not realized what was about to happen. Frank, on the other hand, had realized his position full well and no sound escaped him as he was thrown into the water.

In falling, Jack was thrown clear of the machine, which struck the water with a great splash. Not so Frank, who, held in by the wheel, was carried down with the plane. The lad was very close to death at that moment and he knew it.

He had caught a deep breath as he was drawn under, however, and this stood him in good stead. Calmly the lad reached for the large pocketknife he always carried, and with this, under water as he was, proceeded quietly to cut the sides of the craft sufficiently to allow him to escape. And in this he was successful.

At last he was free and struck upward as swiftly as possible. When it seemed that his lungs must burst for want of air, his head suddenly bobbed upon the surface. He gasped as he inhaled great breaths of the fresh air. A boat approached at that moment and he was drawn aboard, where he sank down.

Jack, when he came up from below, had thought first of Frank. Rapidly he scanned the surface of the sea for some sign of his chum or of the wreckage. Seeing neither, he knew what had happened. Taking a deep breath he dived.

It took the lad some time to locate the sinking mass of wreckage below and when he did come upon it there was no sign of Frank. Jack stayed below until he could stand it no more; then rose to the surface. There rough hands seized him and dragged him into a boat.

In vain the lad struggled. He wanted to get loose so he could make another attempt to rescue his friend.

"Frank!" he cried.

"Be still," said a voice kindly. "Frank is safe in the next boat."

Jack uttered an exclamation of relief and lay still, resting from his exertions.

And so they came again to the Queen Mary and were lifted aboard. Frank and Jack clasped hands when they stood on deck and Jack exclaimed:

"By Jove! I thought it was all over when I couldn't find you down there."

"I thought it was all over myself for a minute," said Frank. "That's one time when this old knife of mine helped out. I brought it back with me."

He displayed the knife and patted it affectionately.

"How do you feel?" asked Jack.

"First rate. And you?"

"Fine. Now we want to see Captain Raleigh."

At this moment the third officer approached.

"Captain Raleigh will receive you the moment you have put on some dry clothes," said the third officer.

"But we must see him at once," exclaimed Frank.

"Change your clothes first," said the third officer kindly.

"But——" Frank began.

"I have Captain Raleigh's orders for you to report to him the moment you have changed," said the third officer sharply. "You will hurry, if you please."

Frank could see that there was no use protesting further. He shrugged his shoulders and the two boys made their way to their cabin.

"The big chump," said Frank, as he slipped off his wet clothing. "The whole British navy might be sent to the bottom while we are doing this. What are a few wet clothes?"

"I guess it was the way we went at it," said Jack. "If we had blurted out what we knew——"

"To tell the truth, I've a good notion to say nothing about what I learned," said Frank.

Jack looked at his companion in the greatest surprise.

"Oh, no, you've not," he said at last, as he slipped on a dry shirt.

"Don't you believe I haven't," declared Frank. "I'm mad. I don't like that way of doing things. Now if it had been Lord Hastings——"

"Well, it wasn't," said Jack. "I'm afraid that's one trouble with us."

"What do you mean by that?"

"Why, simply that he allowed us to get too familiar with him. The result is we expect it from others, and when they don't treat us that way we are disappointed."

"That may be it, of course," Frank conceded. "But at the same time, I didn't like the tone of the third officer just now."

"Perhaps I didn't either," said Jack, "but I've got more sense than to show it. As a matter of fact, I suppose we should have obeyed without question."

Frank continued to mumble as he slipped into a dry coat. He picked up his cap and moved toward the door.

"Ready?" he asked of Jack.

"Almost. How's that shoulder?"

"All right. How's your wound?"

"Just a scratch. Didn't even bleed much." Jack picked up his cap and also moved toward the door of the cabin. "Guess maybe he'll let us see Captain Raleigh now," he said. "Come on."

Frank followed his chum.

On deck almost the first person they encountered was the third officer.

"Didn't take you long," he said with a smile.

"That is because we have important news," said Frank.

"Come, then. I'll conduct you to the captain myself," said the third officer.

Frank and Jack hurried after him.

Captain Raleigh greeted the two lads with a smile, as they stood at attention before him.

"You are back really sooner than I expected you," he said quietly.

"Have you learned anything?"

"If you please, sir," said Jack, "I shall skip the details until later. The German high sea fleet will be off the coast of Denmark before midnight!"

"What's that you say?" he demanded.

"It's true, sir," replied Frank, quietly, stepping forward. "The German high sea fleet, in almost full strength, will attack our patrol squadron in the Skagerak, off Jutland, tonight!"

For one moment Captain Raleigh looked at both lads closely. Then he cried sharply, including all in the cabin with his words:

"Follow me!"

He sprang for the bridge!

CHAPTER XIII

PREPARING FOR BATTLE

"Eleven o'clock!"

Jack returned his watch to his pocket.

"Not much time to gather the fleet together," he said quietly to Frank.

"No," was his chum's reply, "but you can rest assured that all can be done will be done."

Captain Raleigh, upon the bridge, had issued orders swiftly. The Queen Mary, which had been heading southward after Frank and Jack returned aboard, was quickly brought about. After several sharp commands to his officers, Captain Raleigh motioned to Frank and Jack.

"Come with me," he said. "You shall tell me what you have learned as we go along."

The two lads followed him.

Straight to the wireless room went the commander of the Queen Mary.

"Get the Lion quickly," he ordered the wireless operator.

"Lion! Lion!" the call went across the water.

There was no reply.

"Try the Indefatigable," was the next command.

"Indefatigable! Indefatigable!" flashed the wireless.

The receiving apparatus aboard the Queen Mary clicked sharply.

"Indefatigable answering, sir," reported the operator.

"Send this," ordered Captain Raleigh, and passed a slip of paper on which he had scribbled rapidly to the wireless operator.

The message read as follows:

"German high sea fleet to attack off Jutland tonight. Inform Admiral

Beatty. Relay message. Am steaming for Danish coast to engage enemy.

Information authentic. Follow me!

(Signed) "RALEIGH."

A short pause and again the receiving apparatus on the Queen Mary clicked sharply.

"O.K., sir," said the operator.

"All right," this from Captain Raleigh. "Call the Invincible."

Again the wireless began to click. Two minutes later the operator reported:

"Invincible answering, sir."

"Send the same message," instructed Captain Raleigh.

It might be well to state here that all these messages were sent in code, for it was probable that a German vessel of some sort might be within the wireless zone and, if able to read the messages as they flashed across the sea, would have communicated with the main German fleet.

One after another now the wireless of the Queen Mary picked up the battle cruisers Defense, Black Prince, Warrior and the super-dreadnaught Warspite, all of which chanced to be within range of the Queen Mary's wireless. The destroyers Tipperary, Turbulent and Nestore also answered the call and were instructed to proceed to the Skagerak at full speed.

And to each vessel, as it answered, the single word "relay" was flashed. This meant that Captain Raleigh wanted the word sent to other vessels of the British fleet not within her own wireless radius. And the answer to this was invariably the same:

"O.K.!"

Still in the wireless room, Captain Raleigh turned to Frank and Jack and said:

"Now, I shall be glad to know how you boys learned this information."

Jack explained as briefly as possible. Captain Raleigh interrupted occasionally as Jack proceeded with his story and when the lad had concluded, he said quietly:

"You have done well, young sirs. England has much to thank you for."

"But will the others arrive in time, sir?" asked Frank, anxiously. "That," said Captain Raleigh, "I cannot say. You may be sure that they will come to our assistance at all possible speed, however."

"But you will not await them there, sir?"

"No; I shall engage the enemy single handed if necessary."

With this Captain Raleigh turned on his heel and would have left the wireless room. At that moment, however, the wireless began to click again, and the commander of the Queen Mary paused.

"For us?" he asked.

The operator nodded.

"Admiral Beatty, aboard the Lion, calling, sir."

"Take his message!"

There was silence for a moment, and then the operator called off the clicks of his apparatus.

"Admiral Beatty wants to know your source of information," he reported.

Captain Raleigh dictated a reply.

Again silence for a few moments; and then the operator said:

"The Queen Mary is ordered to the Skagerak under full speed. Hold the enemy until the arrival of the main fleet. Assistance on the way. Indefatigable, Defense and Black Prince also steaming for Jutland to lend a hand. Open the engagement immediately you sight the enemy."

"Sign O.K.," said Captain Raleigh.

The operator obeyed and heard the operator aboard the Lion repeat his message.

"I guess that is about all we can do," said Captain Raleigh. Again he turned to leave the room and once more paused at the door.

"Keep your instrument going," he ordered the operator. "Pick up any ship that may not have heard the message. Come, boys," this last to Frank and Jack.

The boys followed their commander back to the bridge; thence to his cabin.

The interchange of messages had taken time, and glancing at his watch now, Frank saw that it was after one o'clock.

"Great Scott!" he exclaimed. "I had no idea we had been in the wireless room so long."

Back in his cabin, Captain Raleigh seemed to have forgotten the boys' presence. He was busy for perhaps an hour poring over a mass of charts and other papers. Frank and Jack stood at attention. They were becoming uneasy, when Captain Raleigh looked up suddenly.

"Pass the word for the first officer," he instructed.

Jack sprang to obey and in a moment the first officer of the Queen

Mary was in the cabin.

"Shape your course for Jutland proper," ordered Captain Raleigh.

The first officer saluted and obeyed.

"We'll go back to the wireless room," Captain Raleigh informed the two lads. "I want to keep you boys near me for I may desire to ask a question at any moment."

The lads followed their commander back to the wireless room.

"Any calls?" he asked the operator.

"One coming now, sir."

"Repeat it as it comes."

"Very well, sir. Indefatigable calling."

"Ask her position."

"Five miles south by southwest, sir."

"Inform Captain Reynolds that we shall slow down and wait for him to come up with us."

"Very well, sir."

The operator sent the message.

"O.K., sir, signed, 'Reynolds,'" the operator reported a few moments later.

"Ask her if she has picked up any other vessels."

"Destroyers Fortune and Shark, sir," reported the operator a little later.

"Good. Give Captain Reynolds our position and tell him to keep working his wireless. Tell him we are likely to need every ship we can bring up."

"Very well, sir."

The operator sent the message.

"O.K., again, sir," he reported.

Captain Raleigh passed a slip of paper to the operator.

"On this," he said, "are enumerated the ships that should be somewhere in these waters. Pick up as many of them as you can. As you give the warnings when answered check them off on the list. If any information is asked, call me."

"Very well, sir," replied the operator, taking the slip of paper. "No other instructions, sir?"

"No. Send the same message as you sent to the Indefatigable."

Captain Raleigh motioned Frank and Jack to follow him and left the room.

"I want you two to attend me closely," he informed the lads. "I shall have lots of leg work that must be done from now until we sight the enemy and even after that. You shall act as my orderlies tonight and while the battle lasts."

Frank and Jack were considerably flattered by this. They knew that

Captain Raleigh had been pleased with their work.

They saluted.

"Very well, sir," they exclaimed in a single breath.

"I want one of you to report to the wireless room, room, ready to bring me any message that may come," instructed Captain Raleigh. "The other will stay here. You can suit yourselves about your positions."

"I'll go to the wireless room, then, sir," said Frank.

"Very well. Report to me instantly a message is received."

Frank saluted and took his departure. Jack stood at attention in Captain Raleigh's cabin as the commander of the Queen Mary again plunged into a mass of charts.

Captain Raleigh sprang to his feet and opened his watch.

"Four o'clock," he said. "We won't reach Skagerak until well after six. I am in hopes the Germans will not try to pass through before early morning. We shall be ready for them then."

"How big a fleet have we there now, sir?" asked Jack.

"None, to speak of. Two or three cruisers and a couple of torpedo boats. I believe we have a submarine or two there also, though I cannot be sure of that."

"We'll lick 'em, sir," said Jack, enthusiastically.

Captain Raleigh smiled.

"I hope so," he said quietly.

At that moment the first officer called from the bridge.

"Battleship overhauling us fast, sir."

"Probably the Indefatigable," said Captain Raleigh.

He went on deck. Jack followed him.

CHAPTER XIV

CHANGED ORDERS

At the same moment Frank came running up.

"Indefatigable reports she has sighted us, sir!"

"Good!" exclaimed Captain Raleigh. "I felt sure it was the Indefatigable. Tell her we shall steam slowly until she comes up with us."

Frank saluted and returned to the wireless room.

Now Captain Raleigh gave an order to the first officer.

"Have all hands piped to quarters, Mr. MacDonald."

Instantly, all became bustle aboard the Queen Mary. Men rushed hither and thither; but in a moment order was restored out of the seeming confusion.

Followed by Jack, his first and second officers, Captain Raleigh made an inspection of the giant battleship.

He addressed the different groups of men as he passed and told them what was about to transpire.

"It is likely to be a one-sided battle at first," he told the men quietly, "but I know that none of you will shrink because of that. You have fought against odds before now. You will not mind doing it again."

The men cheered him.

His tour of inspection completed, Captain Raleigh ordered:

"Let each man be served with a good meal and let them have two hours sleep—all but the watches."

The necessary orders were given and a short time later the men were eating heartily. Then they went to their quarters, where some lay down to sleep while others sat in groups and discussed the impending battle.

Shortly after five o'clock Frank and Jack found themselves alone in their cabin, having been relieved of duty for an hour.

"It's going to be a great fight, Frank," declared Jack.

"You bet it is. It will be the greatest naval battle of history, if the bulk of the British fleet comes up in time. Never before has such a vast array of giant fighting ships as will be engaged in this struggle contended for supremacy. In total tonnage engaged and in the matter of armament and complement it will outrival even the victory of Nelson at Trafalgar and the defeat of the Spanish Armada. And the British, as always, will win."

"Let us hope so. But, as you and I know, the Germans are no mean opponents. Considering the fact that, since the outbreak of the war, they have had little opportunity to practise war tactics on the sea and practically no chance at all to practise gunnery, the few battles that have been fought have proven them foemen worthy of the best we have to offer."

"True," said Frank. "Until reinforcements arrive they will outnumber us. I don't know how many to one."

"To my mind it is foolish to engage the German fleet with only a few ships," said Jack. "It won't gain us anything. I believe we should retreat slowly and draw them on."

"I believe that would be a much better plan. We might engage them at long range, running slowly before them. Then, when the main fleet came up, we would take them by surprise."

And even at that moment the same plan was being revolved in the mind of Vice-Admiral Beatty as, in his flagship, the Lion, he steamed swiftly northward.

By this time the battleship Indefatigable had drawn up almost on even terms with the Queen Mary. The wireless of both ships were busy as the commanders exchanged greetings and discussed their plans for battle. A little later, as the Indefatigable drew even closer, Captain Reynolds of the Indefatigable flashed this message:

"I am coming aboard you."

Half an hour later he came over the side of the Queen Mary and disappeared with Captain Raleigh in the latter's cabin. Directly an aide was despatched for Frank and Jack, who made their way to their commander's quarters.

"So!" exclaimed Captain Reynolds, when his eye fell on Jack, "this lad is one of the two who gained this important information, eh? Let me hear your story again, sir."

Jack repeated the account of the adventures he and his friend had had the night before. Captain Raleigh produced the paper the lads had taken from the commander of the German air squadron and the two commanders scanned it together.

"Well, there is one thing in our favor," said Captain Reynolds. "The

Germans will fail to get the air support they are expecting."

"There probably will be other aircraft with the fleet," said Captain

Raleigh.

"Most likely. Probably a Zeppelin or two with them. Fortunate we have these new anti-aircraft guns aboard. They weren't completed any too soon. Raleigh, what ships are in the Skagerak now?"

"Only three, I believe. The Glasgow, Albert and the Victoria, the former a battle cruiser and the latter two torpedo boats. If we can arrive in time there will be five of us. Then, if the Warspite, the Invincible and the cruisers Defense, Black Prince and Warrior come up in time we will be more on even terms."

"Exactly. But the main fleet, farther south, will hardly arrive in time I am afraid; and, by the way, you are wrong in your calculations. The Warspite is with the main fleet."

"Is that so? So, then, is the Edinsburgh, the Tiger, the Peerless, the Terror, the George IV and the Richard?"

"Yes; those, with a dozen battle cruisers and a score of torpedo boats, comprise the main fleet. If they arrive in time, the Germans must either run or be sent to the bottom."

At this moment a message was handed to Captain Raleigh from the wireless room.

"Change in orders," said the commander briefly, after scanning the piece of paper. "We are to engage the enemy at long range and seek to draw him farther into the North Sea. Orders have been sent to the three ships off Jutland to fall back before the approach of the enemy until we can join them, if they sight the enemy before we arrive. If not, we are all to retire slowly. The Invincible, three cruisers and half a dozen torpedo boats will join us soon after dawn. The main fleet cannot arrive until two hours before noon."

"By Jove, Raleigh!" exclaimed Captain Reynolds, "I am better satisfied with those orders. There is more chance of success now. It would have been foolhardy for us to engage the whole German fleet."

"I agree with you."

"Well, I'll get back to my vessel now."

Captain Reynolds arose and extended his hand to his fellow commander.

"In case——" he said simply.

Captain Raleigh gripped the hand. Then he accompanied Captain Reynolds and saw him over the side.

It was now after 6 o'clock. The German fleet was due off Jutland at almost any moment. Captain Raleigh and Jack made their way to the wireless room.

"Get the Glasgow," commanded Captain Raleigh of the operator.

"Glasgow! Glasgow!" went the call.

"Glasgow!" came the reply a few moments later.

This conversation between the two commanders ensued:

"Have you sighted the enemy?" This from the Queen Mary.

"No," from the Glasgow.

"Have any of your consorts picked up the foe?"

"Not yet."

"You received my earlier instructions?"

"Yes. We are holding our ground until we sight the enemy. Then we shall retire. How long before you will come up with us?"

"In your present position, two hours. If you fall back, we shall, of course, be with you sooner. Are you ready for action?"

"Yes; cleared."

"Good. I am giving my men all the rest possible. Goodbye."

"Funny," said Captain Raleigh to Jack, "they should have sighted the enemy by this time."

"It would seem so, sir," agreed Jack.

"Well, they probably will be in sight by the time we come up with the Glasgow," said Captain Raleigh.

But two hours later, when the Queen Mary and Indefatigable came up with the other British ships, no enemy had been sighted yet. It was then almost nine o'clock.

"You are sure you have not miscalculated the time?" Captain Raleigh asked of Frank and Jack.

"Positive, sir," replied the former. "Besides, you have the document relating to the attack."

"True enough. The enemy probably has been delayed. Or perhaps they will await the coming of daylight."

"It would be better if they did, for us, I mean, wouldn't it, sir?" asked Frank.

"Much better," replied his commander briefly.

"Then let us hope that is what happens."

"But I am afraid it won't happen," said Jack. "If the Germans get this far safely, they won't wait for us to overtake them."

"No; you're right there," said Captain Raleigh. "The thing that worries me is that, if they do get by us, they will spread out all over the sea. They will be able to raid the British coast, may succeed in running through the English channel, and then we shall have to round them up all over again. They would scatter over the seven seas."

"Then we've got to lick 'em," declared Frank, grimly.

Captain Raleigh smiled.

"That's the spirit I like to see," he said quietly. "It is the spirit that has carried the British flag to victory against overwhelming odds on many occasions."

"But he is not an Englishman, sir," said Jack with a smile.

"What?" exclaimed Captain Raleigh. "Not an Englishman? Then what is he?"

"American," was Jack's reply.

"Oh, well, it amounts practically to the same thing," declared Captain Raleigh.

"Next to being an American," said Frank, quietly, "I would be English."

The first officer, Lieutenant MacDonald, burst into the captain's cabin at this moment.

"Message from the Glasgow, sir!" he exclaimed. "German battle squadron, steaming at twenty knots, sighted five miles off Jutland, sir!"

CHAPTER XV

THE FIRST GUN

Skagerak, in which the greatest naval battle of history was about to be fought, is an arm of the North Sea between Norway and Denmark. The scene of the battle was laid off Jutland and Horn Reef, on the southern extremity of Denmark.

From the reef of Heligoland, the main German base in the North Sea, to Jutland, is about one hundred miles as the crow flies. Therefore, it became evident that the German high sea fleet must have left the protection of that supposedly impregnable fortress some time before.

That the advance of the German fleet had been well planned was indicated by the very fact that it could successfully elude the British cruisers patrolling the entrance to the mine fields that guarded Heligoland itself. Could a British fleet of any size have got between the German high sea fleet and Heligoland the menace of the German fleet would have ended for all time.

At the moment, however, the British warships were scattered over the North Sea in such a manner as to preclude such an attempt; and the best Admiral Beatty and Admiral Jellicoe could hope for was to come up with the German fleet and give battle, preventing, if possible, the escape of any units of the fleet to other parts of the sea and to drive all that the British could not sink back to Heligoland.

The German dash of one hundred miles across the North Sea was a bold venture and one that the British had not believed the Germans would attempt at that time. British vigilance had been lax or the German fleet could never have gone so far from its base without discovery; and this laxity proved costly for the British; and might even have proven more costly still.

Above the German fleet came a fleet of aircraft, augmented to a great degree by three powerful Zeppelin balloons. Lying low upon the water also was a fleet of German submarines.

As the German fleet approached Jutland on the night of May 31, it was shrouded in darkness. The night was very black and a heavy fog hung over the sea. The night could not have been better for the attempt, which would, in all probability have succeeded, had it not been for the fact that the British had been forewarned.

Forewarned is forearmed; and this fact alone prevented the Germans from carrying out their designs. It is history that the approach of the German fleet had been reported to the commander of the British cruiser Glasgow by an aviator, who had sailed across the dark sea in a hydroplane. Whether the Germans knew that there were but three British vessels in the Skagerak cannot be told, but certainly they believed they were in sufficient strength to force a passage, particularly by a surprise attack, which they believed the present venture would be.

Therefore, it must have been a great disappointment to the German admiral when a single big gun boomed in the distance.

This was the voice of the British battleship Queen Mary, which, taking directions from the Glasgow's aviator, had fired the opening shot, telling the Germans that their approach had been discovered and that the passage of the Skagerak would be contested.

Immediately the German fleet slowed down; for the German admiral had no means of knowing the strength of the British fleet at that point. Hurried orders flashed back and forth. A few moments later three aeroplanes, which had been hanging low above the German fleet, dashed forward.

They had been ordered forth to ascertain the strength of the British.

In almost less time than it takes to tell it they were directly above the British fleet, which, so far, consisted only of five ships of war— besides the Glasgow, an armored cruiser, the Albert and Victoria, torpedo boats, being the Queen Mary and Indefatigable.

As the Germans approached in the air, a hydroplane ascended from each of the British ships and British aviators gave chase to the enemy. One, which had come too close, was brought down; but the other two returned safely to the shelter of the German fleet, where the British dare not follow them because of the presence of a superior force of the enemy.

But the German aviators had learned what they had been sent to learn. They had discovered the strength of the British. Again sharp orders were flashed from the German flagship.

The fleet came on faster.

Captain Raleigh, because of his seniority, had taken command of the small British squadron. He had drawn his ships up in a semicircle, heads pointed to the foe. As his aviators signalled that the Germans were again advancing, Captain Raleigh gave the command that had been long eagerly awaited by the men—a command which the commander of the Queen Mary had delayed giving until the last moment because he desired to give his men all the rest he could.

"Clear for action!" he thundered.

Jack glanced at his watch and as he did so eight bells struck.

"Midnight!"

The exclamation was wrung from Frank.

"And no aid for at least three hours," said Jack, quietly.

As the lad spoke the fog suddenly lifted and gave to the British a view of the advancing German fleet.

"Forward turret guns!" cried Captain Raleigh, "Fire at will!"

A terrible salvo burst from the 16-inch guns in the forward turret.

At almost the same moment the leading German ships opened fire.

The first few salvos from each side did no damage, for the range had not been gauged accurately.

It became apparent now that the German admiral had no intention of risking all his first line ships in this encounter. Apparently he had decided that his smaller vessels were fully capable of coping with the small number of the enemy that was contesting his advance.

From the shelter of the larger ships advanced the battle cruisers. Not a battleship nor a dreadnaught came forward. But the smaller ships dashed on swiftly and presently their guns found the range.

A shell burst aboard the Glasgow's bridge, carrying away nearly the entire superstructure. The captain and his first officer were killed, and many men were injured as huge splinters flew in all directions. Under the command of the second officer, the Glasgow fought back.

A shell from her forward turret burst aboard the closest German vessel and there was a terrific explosion, followed by a series of blasts not so loud. Came fearful cries from aboard the enemy.

And then the whole sky was lighted up for miles around as the German ship sprang into a brilliant sheet of flame. For perhaps two minutes it lighted up the heavens; then there was another violent explosion and the German cruiser disappeared beneath the water with a hiss like that of a thousand serpents.

A cheer rose on the air—a loud British cheer.

"One gone," said Frank, quietly.

"Yes, but only one gone," replied Jack.

"Yes, but it's two o'clock now," said Frank, hopefully.

"About time to begin our retreat then," said Jack.

And the order for retreat came a few moments later.

The five British ships—for all were still able to navigate in spite of the damage that had been inflicted—came about in a broad circle and headed westward.

Then it was the Germans' time to cheer and they did so with a will. It was not often that a British battleship had fled before a German ship or ships and the Germans, since the war opened, had little chance to cheer such a procedure. But now that they had such a chance, they cheered their best Apparently, they had lost sight of the fact that the British were retiring before superior numbers, and that, even in spite of that and the fact that they now were retreating, they still had the best of the encounter so far.

For one German cruiser lay at the bottom of the sea.

The British retreat was slow; and, for some unaccountable reason, the Germans did not press forward as swiftly as they might have done. Whether they feared a trap, or whether the German admiral had determined to await the coming of day before disposing of the enemy, was not apparent. But that he had some plan in mind, every Briton realized.

"The longer he holds off the better," said Frank.

"Right," agreed Jack. "Of course, we probably could run away from them if they pressed us too hard, but we wouldn't; and for that reason he should be able to dispose of us if he came ahead swiftly."

"Wonder why some of these Zeppelins and airships haven't come into action?" said Frank.

"I don't know. Perhaps the Germans are afraid of losing one of them. They probably have other uses for them, for, should they break through here, it is likely they have their plans laid. What time have you?"

"Three thirty," said Frank, after a glance at his watch. "An hour, almost, till daylight. Do you suppose the others will arrive on time?"

"I hope so. It would be better, of course, if they arrived while it is yet dark, for then they might come up unseen. But with their arrival we still will be outnumbered; and, realizing that, the Germans, when the day breaks, will press the attack harder."

"I guess we will manage to hold them till the main fleet arrives in the morning," said Frank, hopefully.

"We will have to hold them," declared Jack.

At this moment the lads' attention was directed to the cruiser Glasgow. Already badly damaged, a second German shell had now burst amidships with a loud explosion.

"And that settles the Glasgow," said Jack, sadly.

He was right. Gamely the Glasgow fought back, but it was apparent to all, in spite of the darkness, that she was settling lower and lower in the water.

"And we can't rescue the men," said Frank. "Remember the admiralty orders. No ship in action is to go to the aid of another. It would be suicide."

"So it would," said Jack. "Poor fellows."

Slowly the Glasgow settled; and for a moment the fire of all the other vessels—Germans as well as British—lulled a bit. All eyes were bent on the sinking ship.

A wireless message was flashed from the Glasgow to Captain Raleigh of the Queen Mary.

"Goodbye," it said. "Hold them!"

After that there was no further word from the doomed cruiser.

The searchlights of both fleets played full upon the Glasgow as she settled lower in the water. She staggered, seemed to make an effort to hold herself afloat, and then sank suddenly.

The duel of big guns broke out afresh.

CHAPTER XVI

THE BATTLE

Dawn.

With the breaking of the intense darkness what a surprise was in store for the Germans!

Back of the four remaining British ships that had at first engaged the Germans, interrupting their dash and holding them in check until the arrival of a force strong enough to engage the foe more closely, came now the relief promised by Vice-Admiral Beatty.

Gathered from various parts of the North Sea, they had steamed toward Jutland, and, arriving there at almost the same time, they had assumed battle formation in the darkness.

That the British were approaching must have been known by the German admiral, for their wireless apparatus had been working unceasingly, telling of their approach, and these signals must have been caught by the German warships, though, because sent in code, they were undecipherable. Nor could the enemy tell, by the sound, just how close the British were.

Captain Raleigh, too, as well as the other British commanders, had known the other English ships were forming some distance back. Toward these they now retreated; and just as dawn broke, and the British sailors obtained their first view of the promised assistance—and greeted the new arrivals with cheers—the British advanced to the attack.

The German admiral, taking in the situation, knew that he still outnumbered the British—that the advantage was still with him. He determined to give battle. He knew, too, that it was only a question of time until the main British fleet would approach and he determined to win the battle before the arrival of new foes. He signalled an advance.

The British fleet was great and powerful—but not so great and powerful as the German by far. As the Queen Mary, Indefatigable and the two torpedo boats fell back, still the center of German fire and still hurling shell, seeking their proper places in the battle line, the other British vessels came on. And presently the Queen Mary and others had gained their places in the formation.

Ahead of the larger ships now—the Queen Mary, the Indefatigable and the Invincible, advanced the speediest of light cruisers—the Defense, the Biack

Prince and the Warrior. Behind these, spread out fan-wise, came the destroyers Tipperary, Turbulent, Nestore, Alcaster, Fortune, Sparrow Hawk, Ardent and the Shark. The Albert and Victoria also had fallen in line, though badly battered by the effects of the German shells during the night.

Then the three battle cruisers advanced; and as the battle opened, far back came the battleship Marlborough, hurrying to join in the struggle.

The German fleet advanced to the attack in a broad semi-circle. The flagship, the Westphalen, a dreadnaught of 18,600 tons, was squarely in the center. To her left was the battleship Pommern and next the Freiderich; to her right the battleships Wiesbaden and Frauenlob. Beyond the battleships to the left were the cruisers Hindenburg and Lutzow, and beyond the battleships to the right the cruisers Elbing and Essen. Torpedo boats, more than a score of them, also spread far on either side.

Directly behind the single dreadnaught and the battleships came a flotilla of submarines, ready to dash forward at the proper moment and launch their deadly torpedoes. Overhead, and moving forward, were the three giant Zeppelins and a flotilla of other aircraft.

Of all the vessels engaged, the Queen Mary was the largest. The Marlborough, advancing rapidly, came next and then the German dreadnaught Westphalen. The British battle cruisers Indefatigable and Invincible were the next most powerful, in the order named, and the other German vessels were by far superior to the British.

Now, as the battle opened with the greatest fury, another British vessel was sighted to the westward. It was the Lion, the flagship of Vice-Admiral Beatty, steaming at full speed ahead.

Over the tops of the three British cruisers, light vessels travelled swiftly toward the enemy, the larger ships opened with their big guns. The range was found almost with the first salvo and shells began to drop aboard the enemy.

The British cruiser Defense, making straight for the German dreadnaught Westphalen, hurled a shell aboard the German flagship that burst amidships. There was a terrible explosion and men were hurled into the water in little pieces. A hole was blown through the upper deck.

But the Defense paid dearly for this act. The forward guns of the Westphalen poured a veritable rain of shells upon the British vessel and in a moment she was wounded unto death.

There was nothing the other vessels of the fleet could do to aid her; and it was plainly apparent that she must sink. But the British tars stuck to their guns and they continued to hurl shells into the German line until the water of the North Sea washed over them.

The Defense was gone.

This left the Black Prince and the Warrior alone before the larger British vessels and they stood to their work gallantly. The fire of both cruisers was centered on the German flagship; and it was plain that if they continued at their work the Westphalen was doomed.

An order was flashed to the German Zeppelins. Two sped forward.

Captain Raleigh of the Queen Mary saw them advancing and the forward anti-aircraft gun was unloosened. The first Zeppelin, flying low, was pierced before it had moved forward a hundred yards; and it fell into the sea between the German battleships, a flaming mass. But the second came on.

Above the Black Prince the Zeppelin paused. Something dropped through the air. There was a flash, an explosion and a dense black cloud rolled across the water. When it had cleared the Black Prince was gone!

The anti-aircraft guns of the Queen Mary and the Indefatigable fired furiously at the Zeppelin; and a few moments later a shot from the latter struck home. The second Zeppelin fell into the sea. By this time the Marlborough had drawn up with the Queen Mary and the other large British ships; and now these advanced majestically.

The first to encounter the weight of their guns was the German battleship Pommern, of 12,900 tons. Raked fore and aft, she was soon ablaze. Her crew leaped into the sea, almost as one man, following an explosion in her boiler room; and the water was dark with bobbing heads.

The Pommern's sister ship, the Freiderich, slowed down and gave assistance in picking up the crew of the former vessel; and while she was engaged in this work no British gun fired at her.

Gradually the Marlborough, the Queen Mary, the Indefatigable and the Invincible drew closer together as they advanced upon the Germans. Shells burst over them with regularity, but so far none had reached a vital spot.

The Queen Mary turned all her forward guns on the Westphalen and raked her fore and aft. In vain the other vessels of the German fleet sought to detract the Queen Mary's fire. Captain Raleigh had started out with the intention of disposing of the German flagship and he was determined not to heed the others until the Westphalen had been sent to the bottom.

It was no easy task he had set for himself, for he now was the center of fire of the whole German fleet—almost. A submarine darted forward to save the Westphalen. The quick eye of a British gunner caught it. He took aim and fired. The submarine disappeared.

With a view to disposing of the enemy immediately, Captain Raleigh ordered that one of the two forward torpedoes be launched.

There was a hiss as the little tube was released. The distance was so close now that a miss was impossible. There was an instant of silence, followed by a terrible rending sound; then a loud blast. The torpedo had reached the Westphalen's boiler room.

Quickly the German admiral and his officers clambered over the side and rowed to the Wiesbaden, where they were taken on board and the admiral's flag run up. The Westphalen was abandoned; and she sank a few moments later.

In the meantime, the British cruiser Warrior, of 13,500 tons, had been sent down by the explosion of a German shell which had reached her magazine. So rapidly had she settled that not a man of her crew escaped. Thus had the three light battle cruisers of the British—the vessels that had shown the way—been disposed of.

At this moment Vice-Admiral Beatty and his flagship, the Lion, entered the battle. The great guns of the flagship roared above the others and the battleship Frauenlob, singled out by her fire, soon sank.

In spite of the German losses, the British, so far, had had the worst of the encounter and the German admiral, despite the loss of his flagship, had no mind to give up the battle. He pushed to closer quarters.

Now the fighting became more terrific. Shells struck upon all ships engaged at intervals of a few seconds apart. Frequently loud explosions were heard above the voices of the great guns; and in most cases these signified the end of a ship of war.

Among the smaller vessels—the torpedo boats—which had singled each other out, the execution had been terrible. Dead and wounded strewed the decks and there was no time for the uninjured to give aid. They were too busy attending to their guns and manoeuvering their vessels.

But the outcome of an engagement such as this could have but one result, it seemed. Outnumbered as they were and fighting as bravely as they knew how, the British were getting the worst of it. Rather than sacrifice more lives and ships, Vice-Admiral Beatty, on the Lion, gave the signal to retire. He was in hopes that the Germans would follow and thus fall into the clutches of the main British fleet which was advancing at full speed and with which Vice-Admiral Beatty had been in communication by wireless.

The Germans accepted the bait as the British drew off slowly; and as they advanced more ships steamed up from the east. It was a second German squadron advancing to the aid of the first.

There was a cry of surprise from the British, for they had not known that there was a second fleet in such close proximity. These new vessels evidently were the reserves the German admiral had been depending upon to turn the tide of battle should his first line ships not be able to overcome the British.

Seeing apparent victory within his grasp, the German admiral signalled his fleet to full speed; so the British retreated more rapidly.

Suddenly there was a terrible explosion to the right of the Queen Mary. Frank and Jack, as well as all others on the Queen Mary, gazed in that direction. The battle cruiser Invincible suddenly sprang into a sheet of flame and parted in half. A German shell had struck her vitals.

A cry of despair broke from the British as the Invincible—the greatest British ship to suffer so far—dived beneath the waves.

CHAPTER XVII

THE MAIN FLEET ARRIVES

It was by a miracle, it seemed, that the Queen Mary, the Indefatigable, the Marlborough and the Lion, now in the front line, had escaped being struck in their vitals by the German shells that flew all about. On the Queen Mary, dead men and wounded men strewed the deck. They were being carried below as rapidly as possible, where the ship's surgeon, with a corps of assistants, was attending to their wounds.

Frank and Jack had been working like demons. From one part of the ship to the other they had been running with orders ever since the battle opened. The heart of each lad was in his throat—not because of fear— but because the British were getting the worst of the engagement. Never before had they seen an enemy fleet stand up to a British squadron of this size and fight. Always before it had been the German policy to run.

But now they were not only standing up to the British, but were giving them a bad thrashing. Each lad realized, of course, that the British were out-numbered and that the weight of guns was in favor of the enemy; but in spite of this they felt that the enemy should be defeated. They cast occasional glances to the west, hoping to catch sight of the main British fleet, which should be drawing near now.

But at nine o'clock there was no smoke on the horizon.

The loss of the Invincible had been a hard blow to the British. As the others retreated now the Germans pressed them closely. A shot struck the Marlborough in the forward turret, exploding her guns there and killing the gun crews. The effect of the explosion was terrible. Men were hurled high in the air and came down in small pieces.

Jack, in the forward turret of the Queen Mary a moment later, was hurled to the deck as a German shell struck one of the guns and blew it to pieces. The lad escaped the rain of steel that descended a moment later, but others in the turret were not so fortunate. Fully half the men there were killed or wounded so badly that they could fight no more.

Jack sprang to one of the guns himself. It was loaded. Quickly the lad sighted it upon one of the enemy ships and fired.

He watched the effect of this shot. It was the German cruiser Elbing at which he had aimed. He saw a cloud of missiles ascend from amidships and knew that the shot had struck home.

Jack forgot all about reporting to Captain Raleigh for further orders, and as the battle raged, he continued to fire one of the big 16-inch guns—he and other unwounded British tars.

Frank had not seen his chum for an hour; and chancing to poke his head into the forward turret, he was surprised to see Jack working like a Trojan with the members of the gun crew.

"Good work, Jack! Keep it up!" he called.

Jack looked in Frank's direction long enough to wave his hand; then turned back to his work.

Came a loud British cheer. "What's happened?" demanded Jack of the man next him, shouting at the top of his voice to make himself heard above the din of battle.

The man shook his head.

"Don't know," he shouted back, "unless the main fleet has been sighted."

"We might have sunk one of the enemy," said another.

As a matter of fact, both men were right.

Two German torpedo boats had gone to the bottom almost simultaneously under well directed British shots; and, far back across the sea, a flotilla of battleships had been sighted.

Apparently the Germans had not yet sighted the British reinforcements, for they continued to press their foes hard.

Four British torpedo boats had been sent to the bottom of the sea. They were the Tipperary, the Turbulent, the Nestore and the Shark. The others gave slowly before the enemy; and a moment later two of those sank—the Sparrow Hawk and the Ardent.

There now remained facing the entire German fleet the Lion, the Queen Mary, the Indefatigable, the Marlborough and two torpedo boats, the Fortune and the Alcaster.

But the German losses had been great. The Westphalen had been sunk.

So had the Pommern and the Freiderich. The Frauenlob had gone to

the bottom and the Wiesbaden, the new flagship, was badly crippled.

As another German torpedo boat sank, the Germans slackened their pace.

The British had a breathing spell.

But the battle was not over yet. The second German squadron had now approached almost close enough to take a hand in the battle. Apparently this Was what the German admiral was waiting for before resuming operations.

It was plainly evident now that the Germans had sighted the approaching British fleet, but at that distance they were unable to make out its strength. The German admiral decided to continue the battle if he could do so with any hope of success.

So, with the second squadron in range, he gave the command to advance again.

The Queen Mary and the Indefatigable bore the brunt of this next attack and for half an hour it seemed that it was impossible for the two ships to live through the rain of shells that fell all about them. But live they did and they gave as good or better than they received.

The German battleship Hindenburg, pierced by half a dozen shells at almost the same time, staggered back and fell out of line. But the British had no mercy on her. Shell after shell they poured upon her; and at last she sank.

The Wiesbaden, the German flagship, pressed hotly to the attack. Although struck in a dozen places and her port side batteries out of commission, she continued to play on the Queen Mary and the Indefatigable with her forward turret guns.

As a matter of fact, it was fortunate for the Queen Mary and the Indefatigable that they had begun to retire; for their forward turret guns had been silenced and the only pieces that they could now bring into play were in the turrets aft.

A shell from the German battleship Lutzow exploded on the bridge of the Marlborough. The bridge was carried completely away and the commander of the ship was killed, as were half a score of other officers. A second shell struck the Marlborough and carried away her steering apparatus. Absolutely uncontrollable now, the Marlborough drifted toward the Lion, with which she almost collided before the Lion could get out of the way.

There was nothing that could be done for her until after the battle, at any rate, and the others left her to her fate. Drifting as she was, the

Marlborough continued her fire; and of a sudden she put a shot aboard the Lutzow in a vital spot.

The Lutzow blew up with a terrible roar. The crew of the Marlborough cheered and waved their hands to their companions on the other British ships.

Apparently this was more than the German admiral had bargained for. With his whole second squadron intact and the British apparently helpless, he had thought to crush these few ships before aid should reach them; and then, if the approaching British were not too formidable, to offer them battle also.

Now there were only three British ships in line—the Lion, the Queen Mary and the Indefatigable—and these were really not fit nor able to continue the fight.

But the men fought on doggedly. None of the others had thought of surrender and no such idea entered the head of a single man aboard any of the British ships. Help was at hand and then the Germans would get the thrashing of their lives, the men told themselves. They would keep the Germans busy until this help arrived.

Hardly a man aboard the Queen Mary that had not been wounded. Sweat poured from their faces, hands and body as they continued to fight their guns; and as they fought they shouted and yelled encouragement to one another.

"Boom!"

There was a different tone to this deep voice and every man on board the hard pressed British ships knew what it meant.

The first ship of the main British fleet had come within range and had opened with her biggest gun.

Other new voices took up the challenge and within a few moments the roar of battle was at its height once more.

Still a considerable distance away, the dimensions of the approaching British fleet now became apparent to the German admiral. He had thought, at first, that perhaps the newcomers would number a few ships, attracted by the sounds of battle, but as he looked at the formidable array now bearing down on him he knew that his plans, whatever they were, had been frustrated.

"And we had it all planned so carefully," he said between clenched teeth.

He strode up and down angrily, beating the palm of one hand with a knotted fist.

"How could they have learned of it?" he cried. "How could they?"

He was very angry. An officer approached him.

"Shall we draw off, sir?" he asked, and pointed to the fresh British ships bearing down on them.

"No!" thundered the admiral. "Why don't you sink those three ships ahead of you there? Sink them, I tell you!"

The officer saluted and moved away.

For some moments the German admiral continued to talk to himself in great anger; then he suddenly cooled down. With a finger he summoned the officer who had accosted him a moment before. The officer approached and saluted.

"I forgot myself a moment ago," said the admiral. "You may give the signal to retire!"

A moment later the big German ships began to come about; and from the decks of the Queen Mary, the Lion and the Indefatigable there came loud British cheers.

The Marlborough, still helpless, poured shell after shell upon the enemy.

Some distance away still, the British fleet was approaching in an endeavor to intercept the retreat of the enemy. Captain Raleigh of the Queen Mary took in the situation at a glance.

"They'll never do it!" he exclaimed.

He determined upon a bold step. He gave command to bring the Queen Mary about. Then, disabled as his ship was, he started in pursuit of the enemy.

There was a cheer from the Indefatigable, and presently the head of that vessel also came about She started after the Queen Mary!

CHAPTER XVIII

THE SINKING OF THE "QUEEN MARY"

Perceiving this move by two vessels that he believed the same as at the bottom of, the sea, so far as fighting purposes went, the German admiral became very angry again.

"A blight on these English!" he exclaimed. "Don't they know when they are beaten?"

Certainly it seemed not, if the Admiral's version that they were defeated was correct.

The Queen Mary and the Indefatigable steamed after the enemy at full speed.

Jack had relinquished his duties in the gun turret to more experienced hands and had joined Frank on deck. To some extent the forward turret had been repaired and was now in condition to hurl more shells after the fleeing enemy.

It was well after noon when the Germans fled; and as the two British ships followed close on the heels of the enemy—with the main British fleet still some distance back—one of those deep impenetrable fogs that often impede progress on the North Sea suddenly descended.

It was indeed a boon to the fleeing Germans, for without its aid, there is little likelihood that they could have escaped the British fleet, which had the heels of the enemy. But the fog blotted the foe completely from the sight of the main British fleet; and even from the decks of the Queen Mary and the Indefatigable, much closer, it was impossible to make out the whereabouts of the Germans.

The British continued to fire ahead into the fog, but with what result it was impossible to tell.

The fog became more dense until it was impossible to see ten yards ahead. Even the great searchlights on the vessels failed to penetrate the gloom.

"Well, I guess that settles it," said Frank.

"Looks that way," Jack agreed. "These Germans are pretty slippery customers anyhow. It's impossible to catch them in the dark."

"This fog descended as though it were all made to order for them,"

Frank complained.

"Pretty hard to beat a fellow when the elements are fighting on his side," Jack admitted. "I imagine Captain Raleigh will give up the chase now."

But Jack was wrong, though, as it turned out, it would have been a great deal better for all concerned if the chase had been abandoned at that point.

After some conversation with Captain Reynolds of the Indefatigable by wireless, Captain Raleigh announced that the pursuit would be continued and ordered full speed ahead in the deep darkness.

As the vessel gathered momentum, Frank exclaimed:

"I don't like this. I feel as though something disastrous was about to happen."

"Another one of those things, eh?" said Jack, grinning in the darkness that enveloped them.

"What things?"

"I never can remember what you call them. Premonitions, I mean."

"You mean a hunch," said Frank, quietly. "Yes, that's just what I have —a hunch."

"Take it to Captain Raleigh. Maybe he will give you something for it," said his friend.

"This is no joking matter," declared Frank. "I'm not naturally nervous, as you know, but right now my nerves are on edge."

"Just the after effects of the battle," said Jack, quietly. "You are all unstrung."

"I'm unstrung, all right," Frank admitted, "but the battle had nothing to do with it. I tell you something is going to happen."

"Well, what?"

"I don't know."

"It's a poor hunch, unless it will tell you what is going to happen," declared Jack.

"Have it your own way," said Frank. "But wait."

"I'm waiting," said Jack, cheerfully.

The Indefatigable also, following Captain Reynold's wireless conversation with Captain Raleigh, had dashed after the retreating Germans at full speed.

Gradually, although in the darkness neither their commanders nor anyone else on board realized it, the Queen Mary and the Indefatigable, dashing ahead at full speed as they were, were drawing closer together at every turn of the screws.

Frank's forebodings were about to bear fruit.

Now, in the darkness, the vessels were running upon about even terms, but the bows were both pointed toward an angle that would drive them together in collision about a mile distant. Although none realized it, this is what would happen unless the fog lifted suddenly.

But the fog did not lift.

Frank, try as he would could not shake off his spell.

"I tell you." he said again to his chum, "something is going to happen —and it's going to happen soon."

There was so much force behind Frank's words—the lad seemed in such deadly earnest—that Jack grew alarmed. He had had some experience with these premonitions of Frank's.

"What is it?" he asked anxiously.

"I wish I knew," said Frank. "I——"

Came a sudden shout forward; a cry from the bridge. Instinctively,

Frank threw out a hand and grasped Jack by the arm.

Another series of startled cries, the tinkling of a bell in the engine room; a shock as the engines were reversed—but it was too late.

The two British warships came together with a terrible crash!

So great was the force of the shock that Frank, standing on the far side, was thrown clear over the rail. But the lad's grasp upon his chum's arm was so tight that it dragged Jack along with him; and the two boys fell into the sea together.

Aboard both British ships all was confusion now. With startled cries, men rushed on deck. Unable to see in the dense fog, they became panic stricken. While these same men would have faced death bravely in battle, they were completely bewildered at this moment.

In vain the officers aboard both vessels sought to bring some semblance of order out of the confusion. Something had gone wrong with the electric lighting apparatus on both vessels. There was no light. The fog was as thick as ever. The crews stampeded for the rails, but at the rails they hesitated, for they did not wish to throw themselves into the great unknown.

Next came the stampede for life preservers. Men fought over their possession, whereas, in cooler moments, hardly a man aboard either ship who would not willingly have given the life preservers to companions.

Had the men thrown themselves into the sea immediately, it is likely that many of them would have been saved; but their hesitation cost them dearly.

In vain did the reversed engines of both ships work. The sharp steel bow of the Indefatigable had become so firmly embedded in the side of the Queen Mary that it could not be unloosened.

And so the two battleships sank, together in their last moments as they had been when they had faced almost certain destruction under the muzzles of the great German guns such a short time before.

Now men from both ships hurled themselves into the sea in an effort to cheat the waters of their prey. Commanders and officers, however, realizing that there was no hope of life even in the sea, so swiftly were the ships sinking, stood calmly on the bridges and awaited the end. For, they realized, the suction would be so strong when the vessels took their final plunge, that all those anywhere near in the water would be drawn under.

Captain Raleigh sent a hail across the water in a loud voice.

"Are you there, Reynolds?"

"Right here, Raleigh," came back the response. "There is no hope here.

How about you?"

"No hope here either," was Captain Raleigh's answer.

"Goodbye, then," shouted Captain Reynolds.

"Goodbye, old man!"

They were the last words spoken by these two old friends, who had been boys together, schoolmates and bosom companions.

Suddenly the two ships took their final plunge. Men still on board, those of the crew who had been frightened and had not cast themselves into the sea, straightened instinctively as they felt the vessels give beneath them. In the presence of death—when they knew it had arrived— they were as brave and courageous as in the midst of battle.

So there was silence aboard the Queen Mary and aboard the Indefatigable as the waves parted for their coming. All on board, officers and members of the two crews as well, stood calmly, waiting for the dark waters to close over them.

The two ships made a last desperate effort to resist the call of the sea. They failed. A moment later they disappeared from sight. No sound came from the depths.

When Frank and Jack had felt themselves in the water, the latter, realizing immediately what would happen if the ships sank before they had put some distance in between them, struck out swiftly toward what he felt to be the south, giving Frank a hand as he did so.

The latter recovered himself a moment later, however, and gasped.

"I'm all right, Jack. Let me swim for myself."

"All right," said Jack, "but keep close beside me. We'll have to hurry or we shall be pulled under by the suction when the ships sink."

Keeping close together they swam with powerful strokes.

And so it was that they were out of harm's way when the two ships disappeared from sight with a deafening roar as the waters closed over them; they were beyond reach of the suction.

"There they go," said Frank, sadly.

"And it is only a miracle that prevented us from going with them," said

Jack.

"We might as well have gone as to be in the middle of the North Sea," said Frank.

"Nonsense. While there's life there's hope."

They swam on.

Suddenly Jack's hand came in contact with something in the darkness.

"A man!" he exclaimed.

"What did you think I was? A fish?" came the reply. "I've a right to escape as well as you."

"Who are you?" asked Frank.

At that moment, as suddenly as it had descended, the fog lifted.

Jack looked at the other man in the water and uttered an exclamation of pleasure.

"Harris!" he cried.

CHAPTER XIX

ADRIFT

The great naval battle of Jutland was over.

The British fleet now had given up pursuit of the fleeing Germans and Vice-Admiral Beatty paused to take stock of his losses; and they were enormous.

Three great battle cruisers had gone to the bottom—the Queen Mary, of 27,000 tons; the Indefatigable, of 18,750 tons, and the Invincible, of 17,250 tons. Cruisers lost included the Defense, of 14,600 tons; the Black Prince; of 13,550 tons, and the Warrior, of 13,550 tons. The giant battle cruiser Marlborough, of 27,500 tons, had been badly damaged, as had the Lion and other vessels. The destroyers Tipperary, Turbulent, Nestore, Alcaster, Fortune, Sparrow Hawk, Ardent and Shark had been sunk. Total losses ran high into the millions and in the number of men above 7,000.

The German losses had been less, but nevertheless, taking into consideration damage done to the effectiveness of the two fleets as a whole, the enemy had sustained the harder blow. The British fleet still maintained control of the North Sea, while the Germans, because of their losses, had been deprived of a large part of the fighting strength of their fleet. The British, in spite of their heavier losses, would recover more quickly than could the enemy.

The dreadnaught Westphalen was the largest ship lost by the Germans. It was of 18,600 tons. The three German battleships lost, the Pommern, the Freiderich and the Frauenlob, were each of 13,350 tons. Four battle cruisers had been sent to the bottom. They were the Elbing, the Essen, the Lutzow and the Hindenburg, each of 14,400 tons. The German losses in torpedo destroyers had been particularly heavy, an even dozen having been sent to the bottom. Besides this, the enemy had lost three submarines and two Zeppelin airships, besides a number of smaller aircraft. In men the Germans had lost slightly less than the British.

And so both British and Germans counted the battle a victory; the

Germans because in total tonnage sunk they had the best of it; the

British, because they held the scene of battle when the fighting was

over and because the enemy had retired.

But, no matter with which side rested the victory, there was no gainsaying the fact that the battle of Jutland was the greatest naval struggle of all time.

After giving up pursuit of the enemy, the British withdrew. Damage to the various vessels was repaired as well as could be done at sea and the ships in need of a more thorough overhauling steamed for England, where they would go into dry-dock. The bulk of the British fleet, however, still in perfect fighting trim, again took up the task of patrolling the North Sea, that no German vessels might make their escape from the fortress of Heligoland, for which point the enemy headed immediately after the battle.

In spite of the severe losses of the Germans, the return of the high sea fleet to Heligoland was marked by a grand ovation by the civil population. Various reports were circulated on the island, and all through Germany for that matter. One report had it that the entire British fleet had been sent to the bottom; and Berlin, and all Germany, rejoiced.

But as time passed and the German fleet still remained secure behind its fortifications, the German people began to realize that the victory had not been so great as they had been led to believe. They knew they had been fooled; and they vented their anger in many ways.

Street riots occurred in Berlin and in others of the large cities. The people demanded to be told the facts. Later they were told, in a measure, but even then they were denied the whole truth. So conditions in the central empires grew from bad to worse.

Jack and Frank, struggling in the water where they had been hurled by the collision of the Queen Mary and the Indefatigable, were glad of the company of Harris, who had bobbed up so suddenly alongside of them in the darkness.

Harris greeted Jack's exclamation of surprise with a grin.

"Yes; it's me," he replied, discarding his grammar absolutely; "and I'm glad to see you fellows again. Question is, what are we going to do now?"

"Well, you know as much about it as I do," declared Jack. "I haven't any idea how far we are from shore, but I am afraid it is farther than we can swim."

All three cast their eyes over the water. There was not a spar nor other piece of wreckage in sight. But Jack made out a few moments later, some distance to the east, what appeared to be a ship of some sort. He called the attention of the others to it.

"Suppose we might as well head in that direction, then," declared

Harris.

"Right," agreed Frank.

He struck out vigorously and the others did the same.

It was a long ways to that little speck on the water and the lads knew that if the vessel were moving away from them they probably would be lost. But at that distance the vessel seemed to be stationary, so they did not give up hope.

Half an hour later Frank exclaimed: "We're making headway. Ship must be standing still."

"Well, I wish it would come this way," declared Harris. "We're still a long way from safety."

"It's probably a German, anyhow," said Jack, "so if we are rescued it will be only to be made prisoners."

"That's better than being made shark bait," said Harris; "and, by the way, speaking of sharks, I have heard that there were many of them in these waters."

Frank shuddered; for he had a wholesome disgust for the man eaters.

"Hope they don't smell us," he said.

"And so do I," agreed Jack. "We couldn't hope to fight them off, for we have no arms."

"I've got a knife," said Harris, "but I am afraid I wouldn't know what to do with it should a shark get after me."

The three became silent, saving all their strength for swimming.

An hour later they had drawn close to the vessel.

"It's a German all right," said Jack, regretfully.

"Any port in a storm," said Harris. "That talk of shark a while back made me feel sort of squeamish. I want to get out of this water."

They continued to swim toward the ship.

"Wonder what's the matter on board?" exclaimed Frank, suddenly.

They had approached close enough now to see men rushing hurriedly about the deck. Hoarse commands carried across the water, though the words were unintelligible to the three swimmers at that distance.

"Something wrong," said Jack, quietly.

"That's what I call hard luck," declared Frank. "Here we think we have reached a place of safety and something goes wrong."

"Don't cry till you're hurt, youngster," said Harris, quietly. "The ship is there and we're pretty close to it. Those fellows aboard, German or English, are bound to lend us a hand."

"I'm not so sure about that," declared Frank.

"Well, I am," said Harris. "The German sailor is all right. It's the

German officer who makes all the trouble. They'll help us if they can."

The three swimmers were a short distance from the ship now.

Jack raised his voice in a shout.

"Help!" he cried in German.

There was no move aboard the German vessel to indicate that the lad's cry had been heard.

"Told you so," said Frank.

"Don't cry too soon, youngster," said Harris. "We'll try it again, and all yell together."

They did and this time their cries were heard.

Several men aboard the German vessel stopped their rushing about and gazed across the sea in the direction of the swimmers. One man produced a glass and levelled it in their direction. Then he turned to the others and they could be seen to gesticulate excitedly.

"One wants to save us and the others don't," declared Frank.

For some moments the men continued to argue. One shook his finger in the faces of the others and pointed in the direction of the swimmers.

"You're all right," declared Frank, speaking of the one man. "Wish I were there to lend you a hand. But I'm afraid the others are too much for you."

At this juncture the man who opposed the others produced a revolver and made an angry gesture. He was ordering the others to the aid of the three friends in the water.

"By Jove!" said Harris. "He's all right. I'd like to be able to do him a good turn."

And the chance was to come sooner than he expected.

Apparently the men aboard the German vessel had decided to obey the order of the man who would save the three swimmers. A boat was lowered over the side.

Three men stood ready to leap into it. The hopes of the three friends in the water rose high; but they were shattered a moment later in a sudden and unexpected manner.

A dull rumbling roar came suddenly across the water. Instantly all became confusion aboard the German vessel. Officers shouted hoarse commands and struck out with the flat of their swords as members of the crew rushed for the rails.

"An explosion!" cried Frank. "Swim back quickly."

The others understood the significance of that strange rumbling aboard the German vessel as quickly as Frank, and turning rapidly, they struck out as fast as they could.

An explosion such as that dull roar indicated could have but one result and the lads knew it. Evidently there had been a fire on board—that accounted for the strange activities of the men on the ship—and the flames had reached the vessel's magazine.

A second and a louder roar came now. Men jumped into the sea by the scores and struck out vigorously that they might not be pulled under by the suction when the ship sank.

Then there came an explosion even louder than the rest. The great ship parted in the middle as though cut by a knife. A huge tongue of flame shot high in the air. Hoarse cries from aboard, screams and frightful yells. Split in twain, the vessel settled fore and aft.

A second huge tongue of flame leaped into the sky; and then the vessel disappeared beneath the sea.

Giant waves leaped in the direction taken by Jack, Frank and Harris. The sea churned angrily about them and the three had all they could do to keep their heads above water. Then the water calmed down. Frank looked around and there, not fifty feet away, rolling gently on the waves, was the small boat so recently lowered over the side of the German vessel.

With a cry to the others to follow him, Frank turned about and headed for the boat with powerful strokes.

CHAPTER XX

FRIENDS AND FOES

There was reason for Frank's haste.

Swimming close together and bearing down upon the boat from the opposite direction—almost as close from their side as Frank was from his—four German sailors were racing.

They espied Frank and his friends at almost the same moment Frank saw them. One uttered a cry and the others redoubled their efforts to beat Frank to the boat.

Jack and Harris took in the situation quickly. It was then that Jack exerted himself to the utmost. His great, powerful strokes sent him skimming through the water as lightly as a denizen of the deep. A dozen strokes and he had passed Frank. A few more only, it seemed, and he laid hold of the boat and drew himself aboard. Standing erect he looked around quickly. Then, stepping forward, he picked up an oar. He moved to the side of the boat where the Germans were approaching and raised the oar aloft.

"Keep off there!" he cried.

The Germans uttered exclamations of alarm; but they came closer.

"Keep back!" cried Jack, again.

"But you won't let us drown!" exclaimed one of the enemy.

"You stay there until my friends get aboard. Then I'll see what I can do for you," replied Jack.

With this the Germans were forced to be content; for they realized that Jack held the upper hand. It would be impossible for them to climb aboard while the lad stood there brandishing that oar.

Frank laid hold of the boat a moment later and clambered over the side.

Harris was close beside him. Jack called a consultation.

"There is plenty of room for those fellows in here," he said, "but— shall we let them in?"

"We can't see them drown," said Frank. "Still, there is no telling how long we shall be here. Is there sufficient water and food to go around?"

"I'll have a look," said Harris. "Enough for seven of us for about one drink apiece," he said, after an exploration. "There is no food."

"Well, what shall we do?" said Jack.

"Let them come aboard," said Frank. "We can't see them perish without raising a hand to help them."

"And yet they would not have helped us a short time ago," said Jack.

"One man would have helped us," said Harris. "Perhaps he is one of these."

"No, he's not," said Jack. "I would know him in a moment if I saw him.

I obtained a good look at his face."

"Let them in anyhow," said Harris.

"All right," said Jack. He called to the men in the water. "You fellows climb aboard here, one at a time; and when you get in, remember you are our prisoners. Any foolishness and we'll pitch you back again."

The Germans offered no protest and climbed into the boat one at a time.

"Sit in the back, there," said Jack.

The men obeyed.

"Now," said Jack, "I'll tell you where we stand. Water is scarce and there is no food. We shall have to make for shore immediately. I'm in command of this boat and you will have to obey me. Get out the oars and row as I tell you."

The Germans grumbled a bit but they obeyed.

"No time to waste," said Jack, briefly. "We'll head south."

He gave the necessary directions and the boat moved off.

"Help!" came a sudden cry from the water.

Jack looked in the direction of this sound. A single head came toward them, swimming weakly.

"Ship your oars, men," said Jack.

There came a grumble from one of the Germans.

"There is no more room," he declared.

"No," agreed a second. "There is not enough water now. Why should we let another man in the boat?"

"Stop that!" said Jack, sharply. "Cease rowing!"

The men made no move to obey. Jack stood up in the boat and stepped forward.

"Did you hear me?" he said quietly, though it was plain to Frank that he was very angry. "Cease rowing!"

"But——" began the nearest German.

Jack wasted no further time in words. His left arm shot out and he grasped the nearest German by the coat. Raising him quickly to his feet, he struck him heavily with his right fist and then released his hold. The man dropped to the bottom of the boat and lay still.

"Any more?" asked Jack. "Cease rowing!"

The remaining three Germans shipped their oars without a word, although each bestowed an evil glance upon the lad. Frank, catching the look in their eyes, muttered to himself:

"They'll bear watching."

"Harris," said Jack. "That man in the water is the one who would have saved us a short time ago. He seems to be weak. Slip over the side and lend him a hand, will you?"

Harris did so without question and a moment or two later the German tumbled into the boat, where he lay panting, blood streaming from an open wound in his forehead. Harris climbed back in the boat.

"Bandage him up as well as you can and give him a few drops of that water," said Jack.

For his part, Jack stooped over the German soldier he had so recently knocked unconscious and raised him to a sitting posture. Reaching over the side of the boat the lad wet his handkerchief and applied it to the German's head. Soon the man recovered consciousness.

"A drop of water here, too," said Jack, quietly.

"Say," said Harris. "This water is precious scarce. We'll need it ourselves."

"But this man must have a little," said Jack. "Pass it along."

Harris did not protest further and Jack allowed the German soldier to moisten his tongue.

"Now get back to your oars," the lad commanded.

The German did as commanded and soon the little boat was leaping lightly over the waves.

"Take the helm, Frank," said Jack.

Frank relieved Harris, who had been performing this duty.

"Got your pocket compass, Frank?" asked Jack.

"Yes."

"Keep your course due south, then."

"All right, sir," said Frank, with a smile.

"Harris," said Jack, "I want you to stand guard over these sailors for a few minutes. I want to have a talk with our latest arrival. I'll be with you in a few minutes."

Harris stepped forward.

"Ought to have a gun, I suppose," he said.

"I guess not," said Jack. "You and I together should be able to hold these fellows in check."

"Sure; unless they hit us over the head with an oar when we're not looking."

"But one of us must always be looking," said Jack, quietly.

"Well, that's not a bad idea. I'll keep my eyes open."

Jack moved to the side of the German who had been the last to get into the boat. His wound had been bound up as well as possible under the circumstances and he sat quietly, looking out over the water.

"What vessel was that?" asked Jack.

"Hanover" was the reply.

"What was the trouble?"

"Shot pierced our boiler room in the battle. Returning, we were lost from the main fleet in the fog. Our wireless wouldn't work. Fire broke out and we were unable to check the flames. When they reached the magazine she exploded."

"I see," said Jack. "It's fortunate you weren't drawn under with the ship."

"I was," said the German, briefly.

"What?" exclaimed Jack.

"Yes. I was drawn under. I thought I was done for. But, under the surface of the sea there was a second explosion. I felt myself flying up through the water and then I shot into the air. When I came down I was not far from your boat. I called for help."

"By Jove! you have had an experience few can boast of," said Jack. "I wouldn't care to go through it."

"Nor I—again," said the German.

"Now," said Jack, "perhaps you can tell me the nearest way to shore."

The German considered.

"I am not a navigator," he said, "I was only a minor officer aboard the Hanover. But I heard the captain say we were almost 100 miles from the nearest coast line. I am afraid you will not be able to make it in this boat, if your water is as scarce as you say."

"By Jove!" said Jack, "we've got to make it. We don't want to drown out here."

"It's not always what we like," said the German officer, sententiously.

"That's true enough," agreed Jack, "but I have a feeling I was not born to be drowned. We'll find a way out."

"I hope so. However, should you go ashore directly south of here you would be within German lines and you would be made a prisoner."

"Can't help that," said Jack. "I'd much rather be a live prisoner than a dead sailor."

The German smiled in spite of his wound, which, it was plain to all, was giving him great pain.

"Of course," he said, "there is always the possibility of a passing ship."

"That's what we thought before," said Jack. "When we saw your vessel we thought we were safe. But you see how it turned out."

"Well, you'll just have to select a course and stick to it," said the German. "By the way, these men of mine. You are likely to have trouble with them. In our present situation I do not consider that we are enemies, so if the worst comes you may count on me to help you."

"Thanks," said Jack. "I shall remember that."

And the trouble was to come sooner than could have been expected.

One of the German soldiers suddenly laid down his oars.

"I want a drink!" he exclaimed. "I'll row no more until I have a drink!"

CHAPTER XXI

A FIGHT FOR A BOAT

As by a prearranged signal, all four of the Germans threw down their oars and jumped to their feet. Harris, at that moment, in spite of Jack's warning, had been gazing across the sea absolutely unconscious of his surroundings. He was lost in thought.

Frank, at the helm, uttered a cry of warning even as the closest German leaped for Harris and the latter wheeled quickly. He dodged just as the man struck out with a knife he had drawn.

"Want to cut me up, do you?" muttered Harris.

In spite of the wabbling of the boat he fell into an attitude of defense—the old fighting form that had won for him the championship of the British navy in the squared circle. He didn't advance, for he wasn't certain of his footing, the boat pitched so, but he felt fully able to take care of himself.

It was characteristic of him that he made no cry for help. He knew that Jack must have heard Frank's cry of warning. He knew that he would get all the assistance it was in Jack's power to give; and he felt that if Jack were unable for any reason to aid him he must, nevertheless, give a good account of himself.

When Harris evaded the first blow, the German, caught off his balance, pitched forward against him. Harris was almost toppled over, but he threw his left arm around the man's neck and aimed a vicious blow at him with his right fist.

The German's knife arm, because of Harris' hold, dangled helpless at his side. In vain he sought to get it in position where he could drive the point into Harris' body. Harris realized the man's intention. With a sudden move, he pushed the German from him and struck out as he did so. The man staggered back, reeled unsteadily and toppled over the side of the boat with a cry.

The three other Germans rushed Harris at that moment. This time the British sailor was not caught off his guard, and he held the men at arm's length for several seconds.

Meanwhile, Jack had leaped forward, crying to Frank as he did so:

"Keep the helm, Frank! We don't want the boat overturned."

Frank obeyed, much as he would have liked to join in the fight.

Jack reached Harris' side and together the two faced the three Germans.

"We've got them, now," said Harris, quietly.

"Men," said Jack, quietly, "unless you return to your oars immediately, we shall be forced to throw you overboard."

There was a snarl from the three men. Suddenly one dropped to his knees and seized Harris by the legs. Caught off his guard, the latter fell to the bottom of the boat and the others leaped on him.

A knife flashed in the hand of one. With a cry, Jack stooped down quickly and seized the man's wrist even as the point of the weapon would have been buried in Harris' back. The lad twisted sharply and the knife went flying into the sea.

"You would, would you!" cried Jack.

He jerked the man to his feet, planted two hard blows on his chin, and as the man reeled forward clipped him once more. One, two, three backward steps the man took and then pitched over the side of the boat.

"Two gone!" exclaimed Jack.

But he was wrong. For the first man who had been knocked into the sea had been revived by the shock of the cold water. Swimming around the boat unobserved, he had come up behind Frank and now reached up and grabbed Frank by the coat. With a cry of alarm, the lad toppled into the water.

Jack heard his friend's cry. Quickly he took in the situation. Harris had regained his feet and seemed capable of disposing of the two remaining Germans. With a cry to Harris, Jack leaped over the side.

Some distance away he saw Frank struggling with the German who had pulled him from the boat and he swam quickly in that direction.

"I'm coming, Frank!" he called. "Hang on to him."

Frank was doing his best, but he had been taken by surprise and the advantage was with his opponent. The German's hand closed about the lad's throat and he was slowly choking him. Even as Jack came abreast of the struggling figures, Frank threw up his hands and the two disappeared from sight.

Jack, greatly alarmed, dived after them.

Below the surface of the water his hands encountered the struggling figures. He seized the first his hand came in contact with and struck upward. Upon the surface again, he found that he had seized hold of Frank.

Keeping his fingers clenched tightly in Frank's coat—that the lad might not be drawn under again Jack aimed carefully at the face of the German, which now was close to him, and struck out with all his strength.

Instantly, the hand on Frank's throat relaxed and the German sank from sight.

By the force of the impact as the blow landed Jack knew that the German would trouble them no more. Supporting Frank with his left arm, he struck out for the boat with his right.

The German officer leaned over the side and lent a hand in dragging Frank's limp body over the side. Jack clambered over after him. Then he took a view of the part of the boat where Harris battled with two of the enemy.

Both of the latter wielded knives and it was plain to Jack that Harris hesitated to come to close quarters with them, as he had no assistance at hand; for he realized that, should he be overcome, the men would have little trouble of disposing of Frank and Jack, as they tried to climb back in the boat. But now that Jack was able to come to his assistance again, Harris made ready for a spring.

Jack saw this move and called:

"Wait a minute, Harris!"

Harris stayed his spring and Jack again advanced to his side. Jack's face was white and his clothing was dripping water. He was very angry and his fingers clenched and unclenched.

"You men," he said in a cold voice, "were given a chance for your lives the same as the rest of us. Now you will either throw down those knives or die."

One made as if to obey, but the other stopped him.

"Wait!" he cried. "He wants us to throw down our knives so they can overpower us."

To the other this seemed good reasoning. Both Germans, still wielding their weapons, drew backward slowly. Jack and Harris advanced as slowly after them.

"Drop them!" cried Jack, again.

Suddenly one of the Germans sprang forward and aimed a vicious blow at Jack with his knife. The move had been so unexpected, retreating as the men had been, that Jack was almost caught off his guard. He sidestepped quickly, however, and avoided the knife.

But in leaping aside he had jostled Harris, who, dodging a blow aimed by the second German, now was thrown off his balance. In vain he tried to catch himself. It was no use. He went over the side of the boat, uninjured, but for the moment unable to lend Jack a hand.

With two foes before him, Jack realized there was not a moment to be lost. He determined to take the offensive himself, in spite of the odds against him.

With a subdued cry of anger, he charged the two Germans, in spite of the violent rocking of the boat. He caught a stabbing wrist with his right hand and twisted sharply even as he drove his left fist into the man's face. There was a cry of pain and the knife clattered to the bottom of the boat. Again and again the lad struck, paying no attention to the second man. Then, with an extra vicious blow, he knocked the German clear of the boat into the sea.

At the same instant, Harris, who was just climbing back into the boat, uttered a cry of warning and Jack turned just in time to dodge a knife thrust aimed at him by the second German.

With only a single enemy before him, a smile broke over Jack's face. He called to Harris.

"Stay back, Harris. I'm going to settle with this man myself."

The German shrank back, and for a moment it seemed that he would throw down his knife and cry for mercy. But if he had such a thought in his mind, he discarded it; he sprang at Jack, fiercely.

Again Jack avoided the thrust of the knife and caught the stabbing wrist in his right hand. Then, bringing all his tremendous strength to bear, he stooped slightly and jerked with his hand.

The German was pulled clear of the bottom of the boat and ascended into the air. Then he shot suddenly forward and cleared the boat by a good five feet.

There was to be one last encounter before the possession of the boat finally came into the hands of the friends undisputed. One of the Germans, revived by the water, had come up aft and laid hold of the boat near where the German officer sat. The latter saw him and shifted his position just in time to avoid being dragged overboard.

He grew suddenly very angry.

"You murderous dog!" he cried.

Rising to his feet he stooped quickly and seized an oar. Before the man in the water could realize his purpose, he had brought the oar down with all his force on the hand that grasped the boat.

With a howl of pain the German released his hold, his fingers shattered by the force of the blow. Without a word the German officer dropped the oar and resumed his seat.

Jack and Harris now approached Frank's side and the former bent over him. Frank was just regaining consciousness. He smiled as Jack asked him how he felt, and asked:

"Did you lick them all?"

"You bet," returned Jack, then turned to Harris. "I suppose we should pick up some of those fellows, if we can. We can't see them drown before our eyes."

"You're too soft hearted for me," declared Harris. "However, whatever you say."

They gazed into the water. There was no German in sight.

"Be ready to jump in the moment a head appears," said Jack.

Harris nodded and the two stood ready to give aid to the first enemy that should appear.

Ten minutes they waited—fifteen. No head appeared above the surface of the water.

"I guess it's no use," said Jack, slowly, at last. "They're gone!"

CHAPTER XXII

PICKED UP BY THE ENEMY

It was dark.

All through the afternoon Jack and Harris had rowed untiringly, but with the coming of nightfall there was no land in sight.

"Nothing to do but keep pulling in the same direction," said Jack.

Harris nodded.

"All right," he said, "but I'm getting tired. I'll have to rest up for an hour or so."

"Let me row awhile," said Frank. "One of you fellows can take the tiller here."

"Feel all right?" asked Jack.

"First rate."

"All right, then," said Jack. "You and Harris change places."

This was done. Then the German officer spoke.

"It's about time for me to take a hand," he said.

"But your wound?" protested Jack.

"Well, it still pains some, to be sure. But the sooner we get to shore the sooner I will be able to have it looked after. It's better to row awhile than to remain idle."

"Suit yourself," said Jack. "I am a bit tired. We'll change places."

They did so and the little boat moved on in the darkness.

"Don't know where we are," said Jack to Harris, "but it seems to me we should raise land with the coming of daylight."

"Well, I hope we do," was Harris' reply. "I'm getting awfully thirsty, but I hate to cut into that water supply."

"There is a little more for us since we lost our other passengers," said Jack. "I'm thirsty myself. We may as well sample that water."

He produced a jug and each took a cooling draught.

"Tastes pretty good," said Harris, smacking his lips.

"You bet," agreed Jack.

He made his way forward and gave Frank and the German officer a drink.

"Enough for a couple of more rounds," he said, shaking the jug and listening to the splash of the water inside.

"Oh, I guess we've enough," said Harris. "However, it is well to use it sparingly."

As it turned out they had an ample sufficiency; in fact, more than they needed.

With the coming of daylight, Frank, who had resumed his place at the helm a short time before, uttered an exclamation.

"Ship!" he cried.

He pointed off to port.

The others glanced in the direction indicated and then raised a cheer.

There, scarcely more than a mile away and bearing down on them rapidly, came a German man-o'-war. Already they had been seen, for the vessel altered its course slightly.

Jack gave a sigh.

"Sorry it's not a British ship," he said.

The German officer was forced to smile.

"And I'm glad it's not," he declared; "for if it were it would be capture for me instead of you."

"But there are three of us and there is only one of you," protested

Frank.

"Well, it's the fortune of war," said the German.

"The misfortune of war in this case," said Harris.

The German warship was now within hailing distance and a voice called:

"Who are you?"

The German officer acted as spokesman and shouted back:

"German officer and three British."

"We'll lower a boat," was the response.

A few moments later a boat put off from the ship, manned by a dozen German sailors. Fifteen minutes later the lads found themselves aboard the German warship, where they were immediately conducted to the cabin of the commander.

The latter turned to the German officer for an account of what had happened.

"So these British sailors saved you?" he said. He turned to the three. "I must thank you in the name of the Emperor," he said, quietly. "Now, if you will give me your paroles, I shall allow you the freedom of this vessel."

The three friends glanced at one another and the German commander smiled.

"I can assure you there is no possibility of escape," he said.

"In that event," said Jack, "we shall give our paroles until we reach shore."

"That is sufficient. After that you will be in other and safe hands."

The German commander summoned a minor officer, to whom he introduced the three friends.

"You will see that they are provided with suitable quarters," he said.

The officer saluted and motioned for Jack, Frank and Harris to follow him. A few moments later the three found themselves installed in comfortable quarters, where clean linen and dry outer clothing Was laid out for them.

"You've got to give them credit," said Frank. "They do things up in style. It seems we are to be well treated."

"No reason why we shouldn't be," declared Jack.

"Wonder where we are bound, anyhow?" said Harris.

"Don't know," said Frank. "I'll try and find out as soon as we can go on deck—providing they allow us on deck."

"The commander said we would have the freedom of the ship," returned

Harris.

"So he did. Hurry and dress then."

Half an hour later, refreshed by a bath and food, the three made their way on deck, where they found the young German officer who had escorted them to their cabin. They approached him and the latter received them cordially.

"Wonder if you would tell us where we are bound?" asked Frank, with a smile.

"Certainly," was the reply. "Our destination is Bremen."

"Bremen, eh?" said Jack. "What will they do with us there?"

"Probably turn you over to the military authorities to take care of you until the end of the war."

"Looks like our fighting days are over," said Harris, sadly.

The young German smiled.

"Seems to me you should be rather glad of that," he returned. "After your defeat off Jutland you should be willing to cry for peace."

"Defeat!" exclaimed Frank. "Why, the Germans got the worst of it. You know that."

"Oh, no we didn't," said the young officer. "The greater part of the

British fleet was sent to the bottom. Our losses were insignificant."

"Were you there?" asked Frank.

"Why, no," said the German, "but——"

"Well, we were there," said Frank. "Therefore, we know something about it. I give you my word that I saw one German dreadnaught, two battle cruisers and four cruisers sunk with my own eyes. Also I saw half a dozen destroyers sent to the bottom and two Zeppelins shot down."

"Impossible!" exclaimed the young German officer. "The official report of the battle gives our losses as two destroyers and a single cruiser, while the greater part of the British fleet was sunk."

"Where is the German fleet now?" asked Frank.

"Back in Heligoland. Some of the vessels are in need of slight repairs."

"Why didn't they keep going after that great victory?" Frank wanted to know.

"Why, I can't say. Probably had orders not to proceed too far immediately."

"I can tell you why," said Frank.

"I wish you would," said the young officer.

"The reason," replied Frank, "is perfectly simple. It's because the main British fleet is out there waiting for you fellows. After we chased your fleet back——"

"But you didn't chase us back. We retired when the battle was won."

"Oh, you retired when the battle was won, eh?"

"Yes; that's what the official report says."

"But it doesn't say who won the battle, does it?" asked Frank, with a grin, in which his friends were forced to join.

The young officer gazed from one to another, and Frank continued:

"Now, I'll tell you something you don't seem to know. We were pursuing the German fleet when two of our vessels crashed in the fog. That's how we happen to be here now."

"But I tell you that is not possible," protested the German.

"It may not have been considered possible," returned Frank, "but it's a fact, all the same."

"You mean, then, that the official report is not true."

"Well, that's my personal opinion of it," Frank admitted.

"Sir!" exclaimed the young German, drawing himself up suddenly. "You have insulted the German navy—and me with it. Were it not that you are our guests aboard this warship, I would demand satisfaction."

"Look here," exclaimed Frank. "I didn't mean to hurt your feelings. I was just telling you the facts in the case. I——"

The young German faced him angrily.

"Your half apology only adds to the insult," he said. "I shall leave you now."

With this he drew himself up stiffly, turned on his heel and stalked away. Frank gazed after him amusedly.

"Now what do you think of that?" he exclaimed.

"You should have known you couldn't convince him," said Jack.

The three friends walked along the deck gazing out over the water. Half an hour later, as they were about to go below, Frank caught sight of a figure in the uniform of a German lieutenant, who was eyeing them closely.

There was something familiar about that figure and unconsciously the lad gave a start. He called Jack's attention to the man, and the latter, seeing that he was the subject of discussion, quickly withdrew.

"I've seen him some place," said Frank.

"And so have I," Jack declared. "There is some thing strangely familiar about him. Say! It's unpleasant when you know a man and can't place him."

"Let's hope he is not some old enemy come back to life," said Frank, quietly, as they returned to their cabin.

CHAPTER XXIII

AN UNKNOWN FRIEND

Bremen. The greatest of all German shipping centers, and, before the outbreak of the European war, one of the greatest seaports in the whole world.

Even on the third day of June, 1916, when the German warship on which Jack, Frank and Harris were prisoners steamed into Bremen the port was alive with activity. Great German merchant ships, useless since the war began, appeared deserted, but other and smaller craft dashed hurriedly hither and yon.

"Why all the excitement?" was Frank's comment, as the three stood well forward while the warship steamed through the harbor.

"Several reasons, I guess," said Jack. "One is that half of these small vessels ply between Bremen and Scandinavian ports in spite of the British blockade; and the other reason probably is the fact that the city is celebrating the great naval victory."

"Naval victory?"

"Sure; the battle of Jutland. The German people have been told that the German fleet won; and now the people are celebrating. See all those flags? Why else would they be displayed so profusely?"

"Because Germany is at war," said Frank.

"Oh, no they wouldn't. You remember we were in Hanover once while the war was in progress. You didn't see all those flags about like that."

"I guess you're right."

At that moment a German officer approached the three friends.

"I've something of interest to show you," he said; "something that will be of interest to all the world presently."

"We shall be glad to see it, whatever it may be," replied Jack, courteously.

"Look over the side there," said the German, pointing. "Do you see that long, low shape in the water?"

"Why, yes," said Frank. "Looks like a submarine."

"That's what it is. Can you make out the name?"

The three friends peered at the object closely.

"D-e-u-t-s-c-h-l-a-n-d," Frank spelled it out.

"Yes, the Deutschland" replied the German officer; "and, within a month, the whole world will be talking about her."

"What's she going to do?" asked Frank. "Sink the whole British fleet?"

The German officer smiled.

"No," he replied quietly. "The Deutschland will be the first of a fleet of merchant submarines to ply between Bremen and the United States."

"What?" exclaimed Jack, in the utmost surprise. "You mean that submarine will try and run the English channel and make for the United States?"

"Exactly."

"But it's impossible," said Frank.

"Not at all," returned the German. "You may remember that German submarines made their way to the Dardanelles safely. The only difference will be that the Deutschland will go unarmed. She will carry a cargo of dyestuffs and other commodities of which the United States is in need."

"Well, she may try it, but I don't believe she'll get there," said

Harris.

"Nor I," declared Jack.

But Frank wasn't so sure. An American, he had not the strong prejudice of his two companions.

"It will be a great feat if she can accomplish it," the lad said.

"It will, indeed," said the German, "and she will accomplish it."

"One thing, though," said Frank, "she won't be able to carry a very valuable cargo. She's too small."

"She'll carry a cargo worth more than $2,000,000," said the German officer, "and in payment she will bring back gold and securities, and you may know that Germany is in need of cash."

"By Jove!" exclaimed Frank. "We'll have to admit that you Germans are progressive. We may not like to admit it, but it's a fact all the same."

"I thank you," said the German with a low bow.

"Well, we're obliged to you for showing us the Deutschland, at all events," said Jack, "and I want to say that if by any chance she does reach the United States you may be well proud of her."

"I second that," declared Harris.

Again the German bowed low.

"Now," said Frank, "as we have passed beyond sight of the Deutschland, perhaps you can tell me what is to be done with us?"

"As it happens, I can," was the reply. "I heard the captain inform Lieutenant von Ludwig that you will be put in his charge. He has instructions to see you safe in the hands of the military authorities in Berlin, where most of the captured British and French officers are being held."

"Pretty tough, Jack," said Frank.

The German officer overheard this remark, although he perhaps did not catch the exact meaning.

"You will be well treated," he said.

"I've no doubt of that," declared Jack.

The German officer left them.

Jack turned to Frank.

"Say!" he exclaimed, "are you thinking of turning German directly?"

"What's that?" demanded Frank, in surprise.

"I just wondered when you were going to take up the arms for the Kaiser. The way you have been praising all things German recently, I don't know what to make of you. The Deutschland, for instance."

Frank smiled.

"I just don't happen to be a hard-headed John Bull," he replied.

"Hard headed, am I?" exclaimed Jack. "I've a notion to shake some of that German sympathy out of you."

"You know I haven't any German sympathies," said Frank. "But I believe in giving credit where credit is due."

"Well, there is no credit due there. You know that is just some cock and bull story. The Germans will never dare such a thing."

"I'm not so sure," said Frank, quietly.

"Well, it will never get across the sea if the attempt is made."

"Maybe not, maybe yes," said Frank, with a grin.

"Well——"

What Jack might have replied Frank never learned, for at that moment another German officer accosted them. He was the man who was so strangely familiar to Jack and Frank.

"You will be ready to accompany me the moment we dock, sirs," he said.

"All right," Frank agreed. "We'll be ready."

They descended to their cabin where they donned the clothing they had worn when picked up from the sea. Then they returned on deck.

The great warship now was nearing the dock, backing in. Slowly she drew close to the pier and then finally her engines ceased. A gangplank was lowered and men began to disembark.

The officer who was to conduct the three prisoners to Berlin tapped

Jack on the shoulder.

"Whenever you are ready," he said quietly.

"We're ready now," returned Jack.

"Then precede me ashore," was the reply. "By the way, I might as well advise you that there is no use of attempting to escape. I have my gun handy and will drop either of you at the first false step."

"Don't worry, we have no intention of trying to escape—not right here in broad daylight," said Frank.

"Very good. Let us move."

Slowly they made their way down the gang plank and ashore. There a line of automobiles waited. The officer motioned his prisoners into the largest of these and gave instructions to the driver. He took a seat beside Jack.

As the automobile started down the street, Jack glanced at his captor sharply.

"Surely I have seen you some place before, sir?" the lad said.

The officer shrugged his shoulders.

"Who knows?" he said and became silent.

"Deuced uncommunicative sort of a fellow," said Jack to himself. "But I know I've come in contact with him some place. It may come to me later."

The automobile drew up in front of a large stone house and the officer motioned his prisoners out. He spoke to his chauffeur.

"Keep your gun handy and follow me," he instructed.

The driver nodded and stepped alongside the officer, who motioned the three friends up the steps ahead of him. Inside he motioned them into a parlor and then dismissed his chauffeur.

"Now," he said, "I want your promises not to try to escape."

"Sorry, sir, but we can't do that," replied Frank, quietly.

"Come! Don't be fools!" exclaimed their captor, sharply.

He walked to the door and peered out. Then, walking close to Frank and

Jack, he said quietly:

"If you will give me your promises to make no attempt to escape before tomorrow night, I shall not have you guarded."

Both lads started back in surprise, for the man had spoken in English and without the trace of an accent.

"Great Scott!" exclaimed Frank. "You must be an Englishman."

The man laid a finger to his lips.

"Sh-h-h!" he warned. "Walls have ears, you know. So you don't know me?"

The lads gazed at him closely.

"I know I have seen you some place," declared Jack.

"So have I," said Frank.

"And to think that they don't know me," said the man, half to himself.

Then he addressed them again.

"I guess it is as well that you have not recognized me, but did I not know you so well I would not say what I am about to say. That is this. I am an Englishman and I am here on an important business. Tomorrow night I shall return to England. Give me your words to remain quiet here until then, in the meantime not trying to learn my identity, and you shall all go with me. Is it a bargain?"

Frank looked at the man sharply. Was he fooling them? Well, the lad decided, they had everything to gain and nothing to lose.

"Very well," the lad said. "You have my promise not to attempt to escape before tomorrow night."

"And mine," said Jack.

"And mine," declared Harris.

"Very well. Then I shall leave you for the moment."

The man stalked from the room and closed the door behind him.

CHAPTER XXIV

THE BOYS BECOME UNEASY

For some moments after the officer had taken his departure, there was silence in the room. Then Harris exclaimed:

"Now what do you think of that?"

"Well, I don't hardly know what to think of it," Jack replied. "Frank took most of the talking on himself. When he gave his parole there was nothing left for me but to do likewise."

"That's what I thought. Otherwise I wouldn't have given mine," said

Harris.

"It may not be too late to call him back and tell him so," said Frank. "I did the talking because neither of you seemed to want to do it. You didn't have to give your parole unless you wanted to. I didn't ask you to do it."

"Come now, don't get mad, Frank," said Jack.

"I'm not mad. I'm just telling you what I think. Certainly it can do us no harm. We have everything to gain and nothing to lose."

"That's so, too, when you stop to think of it," Harris agreed.

"Well, I stopped to think of it," said Frank. "You fellows didn't.

That's the difference."

"But who on earth can he be?" exclaimed Harris. "He seems to know you two, all right."

"There is something strangely familiar about him," said Frank, "but I can't place him."

"Nor I," admitted Jack, "though, as you say, there is something familiar about him."

"Seems to me that if I knew a man I could tell you who he was," said

Harris.

"Seems so to me, too," declared Frank, "but I can't."

"Well," said Jack, "I'm not as credulous as you are, Frank. I wager he is not doing this to help us out. I'll bet we land in Berlin and stay there until the end of the war."

"By Jove! Let's hope not," said Harris. "Still, all things considered,

I'm of your way of thinking."

"If he was telling the truth," said Jack, "he would have let us know who he is. There was no reason for telling us he was English and then concealing his identity."

"I can't see any reason," Frank admitted, "but at the same time I believe he was telling the truth."

The conversation languished. Frank curled himself up on a sofa at the far side of the room and sought a little rest. Jack dozed in his chair. Harris also could hardly keep his eyes open.

They were still in this condition when the door opened several hours later and their captor again entered the room. He walked quickly across the room and shook Jack.

"Hello!" said the latter, sleepily, "back, eh?"

Frank awoke at the sound of Jack's voice and Harris also opened his eyes.

"I had a little work that had to be disposed of immediately," said their captor, "which is the reason I left you so abruptly. I can show you a place to sleep now."

He led the way from the room and upstairs. There he ushered the three into a large, well appointed room, which contained two beds.

"Only two beds," he said, "but it's the best I can do. Two of you can bunk together."

"Anything, just so it's soft," said Frank. "I'm tired out."

"Then you had all better turn in at once," said their captor. "I have much work to do. It is probable that I shall not be back again until some time tomorrow night. Make yourselves at home. You are alone in the house. You will find cold meats, bread and some other things in the pantry down stairs. Remain here until I come."

"Very well, sir," said Frank. "And you say we shall leave here tomorrow night?"

"Yes; unless something develops to interfere with my plans."

"All right, sir. We shall remain here until you come tomorrow night. But that is as long as our paroles hold good, sir. After that, we shall escape if it is humanly possible."

"I will be back before midnight tomorrow," was their captor's reply. "Until that time, goodbye. One thing, stay in the house and keep the blinds drawn. I do not wish to attract attention to this house."

"Very well, sir," said Frank.

The man took a last careful glance around the room and then disappeared.

"Well, he's gone again," said Jack. "He may be telling the truth and he may not, but one thing sure, these beds look pretty comfortable. I'm going to make use of one right now."

He undressed quickly and slipped between the sheets. Frank and Harris followed his example.

All were up bright and early the next day, greatly refreshed. They found food in the pantry, as their captor had told them they would. It was a tedious day, confined as they were, and the time passed slowly. But dusk descended at last.

"He should be here at any time now," said Frank.

The others said nothing, but when nine o'clock had come and gone even

Frank became uneasy.

"Don't see what is detaining him," he said.

"Nor I—if he really meant to come back," said Jack.

Eleven o'clock and still their captor had not returned.

"He said he would be back by midnight," said Frank.

"He said lots of things," said Jack, "but they didn't make the same impression on me they seem to have made on you. I don't believe he is coming."

"I'll tell you what I think," said Harris. "I believe he expected us to make a break for liberty before now. The house probably is surrounded and if we start out the door we shall most likely be shot down."

"By Jove! I wouldn't be surprised if you had hit the nail on the head,"

Jack declared.

"Nonsense," said Frank. "What would be the advantage of a plan like that?"

"Well, I don't know; but there is something queer about this business," declared Jack.

Eleven thirty passed and still no sign of their captor.

Jack and Harris had kept up a steady flow of conversation regarding the probable fate that was in store for them if they poked their heads outside the door, and at last Jack rose to his feet.

"Well," he said quietly, "there is no need of staying here. We may as well make a break for it Chances are, if we are quick enough, we can get into the open without being shot down."

"Not in these clothes," said Harris.

"True enough. We'll have a look for other clothing. What do you say,

Frank?"

"I'm not convinced yet the man is not coming back," said Frank, "but I

tell you what I will do. We'll hunt up some other clothes and get into

them. Then we'll wait until twelve o'clock. If he has not returned by

that time, I'm with you."

"Fair enough," said Harris. "Come on."

The three made their way upstairs, where they started a thorough search of the house; and at last Jack ran onto a closet in which were stored half a dozen suits of civilian clothes.

He called the others.

"All right if they'll fit," said Harris.

Fortunately, they did fit; and fifteen minutes later the three were garbed in plain citizens' attire. They left their uniforms in the room where they had changed.

"Now to see if we can find a few guns," said Jack.

Again they searched the house.

Frank was the first to find a weapon. There were two revolvers in a drawer of a writing desk in the parlor and with them was a goodly supply of ammunition. Frank gave one of the guns to Jack.

"We ought to be able to find one more," said Harris. "I've got to have a gun."

They ransacked the house from top to bottom; and at length Frank came across another weapon. Harris gave an exclamation of satisfaction.

"Let's divide up that ammunition, now," he said.

This was done and the three returned to the parlor. Frank glanced at his watch.

"Five minutes to twelve," he said. "We'll wait until midnight and not a second longer."

To this the others agreed.

"I guess you were right after all," Frank told his companions. "Still I can't understand this thing at all."

"You'll probably understand it better when you stick your head out the door and a bullet hits close to it," said Harris, grimly.

"No; I don't believe there is anything like that going to happen,"

Frank declared. "Maybe he was detained and couldn't get back on time."

"When he gets back he'll find us missing," said Harris.

"He will unless he hurries," Frank agreed.

The minutes passed slowly; but at last the hands of Frank's watch pointed to midnight.

The lad closed the case of his watch with a snap and rose to his feet. He examined his revolver carefully to make sure it was in working order and then said:

"Time's up; may as well be moving."

The three advanced cautiously to the front door. Behind, the house was perfectly dark.

"Careful when you open the door, Frank," Jack warned. "Stoop down.

There is no telling what may be lurking out there."

Frank heeded this warning. Stooping, he opened the door, threw it wide and looked out.

"Coast clear," he announced.

He was about to step out when the sound of hurried footsteps came to his ears.

"Wait a minute," Frank whispered. "Some one coming."

A man appeared down the street. He came nearer. Frank gave an exclamation of satisfaction:

"Come on back to the parlor," he whispered. "Here he comes now."

CHAPTER XXV

TOWARD FREEDOM

Jack and Harris obeyed Frank's injunction and the three flitted back to the parlor silently.

A moment later the front door opened softly and directly the officer appeared in the parlor door.

"I came almost not getting here," he said with a smile. "Did you get tired waiting?"

"So tired," said Frank, "that we were just about to leave when I chanced to see you coming down the street."

"So? Well, you would have had a hard time escaping, I am afraid. Now, my way it will be easier. I have had my means of escape laid out ever since I arrived here. Unless something unforeseen occurs, we should be able to get away without difficulty."

"I am sure I hope so," declared Frank.

Their captor surveyed the three closely.

"I see you are all ready," he said. "Changed your clothes, eh?"

"I hope you didn't think we were going prowling about the street in our

British uniforms?" said Jack.

"Hardly. By any chance did you find weapons, too?"

Frank hesitated. For a moment he debated what was best to answer.

However, the odds were now three against one, so he replied:

"Yes; we have a gun apiece."

"Good; then we may as well be moving. The car should be here in ten minutes at the latest. You see, that's why I was late. Had a blowout aways back. We had to come in on foot. I sent my driver for another car while I hurried here, for I was afraid that you might do something rash. You see, I know more about you than you think I do."

"I wish you would tell us who you are, sir," said Jack.

"All in good time," replied the officer with a smile. "All in good time."

Came a "honk-honk" from without.

"There's our car," said the officer quietly. "Come along."

Without a word the others followed him through the dark hall, out the door and down the steps, where they climbed into the car, in the rear seat, their captor taking his seat with the driver.

The automobile started immediately.

They rode along slowly for perhaps an hour; and they came to what the lads recognized immediately as the water front. Their captor called a halt and climbed out, motioning the lads to follow him. Immediately they had alighted, the automobile drove away.

Straight down to the water their captor led the way. Jack whispered to

Frank.

"You can't tell me we are going to get away from here as easily as all this."

"Sh-h-h!" was Frank's reply.

Jack thereafter maintained a discreet silence.

At the edge of the pier their captor pointed to a small rowboat in the water.

"We'll get in here," he said.

They did so and a moment later they were being rowed across the water by a man Frank recognized as a German sailor. The thing was becoming more complicated.

A short distance ahead there now loomed up what appeared to be nothing more than a motorboat of considerable size. The rowboat approached this craft and the officer motioned his three companions to follow him aboard. They did so.

Aboard, they saw that the vessel upon the deck of which they stood was in reality a pleasure yacht, now converted into a vessel of war. A look at her graceful outlines and long slender body told all three that the vessel was built for speed.

Their captor had halted and waited for the three to come up with him.

"Follow me below," he whispered. "I'll do the talking. Agree with whatever I say and listen carefully to my every word."

The three friends obeyed.

Below they were ushered into what proved to be the commander's cabin.

An officer in the dress of a lieutenant commander of the German navy

rose and greeted the boys' captor with a salute and an extended hand.

Their captor grasped the hand.

"Commander von Ludwig, I take it," said the commander of the vessel.

Von Ludwig bowed.

"The same, sir," he replied. "I have here a paper that gives me command of your vessel, sir. You are ordered to report to Berlin at once."

"I have been expecting you, sir," was the reply. "I shall leave at once, if your boatman is still near."

"I ordered him to await you," was von Ludwig's reply.

The commander of the German vessel glanced at von Ludwig's three companions.

"Your officers?" he asked.

"Yes. Your officers will be relieved in the morning."

"Very well, sir. Then I shall leave you. A safe and successful voyage to you, sir."

"The same to you, sir."

Von Ludwig, motioning to his companions to remain in the cabin until his return, went on deck with the departing commander. A few moments later the latter was being rowed ashore. For the space of several seconds, von Ludwig gazed after him, a peculiar smile lighting up his face as he murmured:

"If you only knew what a time I had getting the paper I just gave you, you would not be going so serenely about your business right now. Oh, well——"

He threw open his arms with a gesture and descended to his cabin.

"Now," he said to Jack, Frank and Harris, "the first thing we must do is to secure the crew and the officers of this vessel. The crew, I happen to know, numbers only ten men. There are two officers. We shall have to overcome them."

"And how are we going to work the ship, sir?" asked Jack.

Von Ludwig glanced at the lad sharply.

"You would be a better sailor, sir, if you would follow orders without question," he said sharply; then added more calmly: "However, I shall tell you, for I can see none of you trust me fully. I have my own crew of five men coming aboard within the hour."

"I beg your pardon, sir," said Jack.

"That's all right," said von Ludwig. "Now follow me."

The others did as ordered. Before a door not far from the commander's cabin von Ludwig stopped.

"In there you will find the first officer," he said

He motioned to Frank and Jack. "Get him and get him quietly."

The lads nodded their understanding and von Ludwig signalled Harris to follow him.

Jack laid his hand on the knob of the door and turned it gently. The door flew open without a sound.

"Find the light switch, Frank," Jack whispered.

Frank's hand felt carefully over the wall.

"Turn it on when I give the word," said Jack. "I may need to see what I am doing."

"All right; but be careful, Jack."

Slowly Jack tiptoed across the room, where he could dimly see a form stretched across a bunk. Bending over the figure, Jack raised a hand and then called to Frank:

"Lights, Frank!"

Instantly, Frank threw the switch and then sprang forward to lend Jack a hand should it be necessary. But his assistance was not needed. Jack's fist rose and fell once and the form in the bunk gasped feebly once and lay still.

"I don't like that sort of thing," said Jack, "but I suppose it had to be done. Help me bind him up and gag him. He's not badly hurt and will come round in a few minutes."

It was the work of but a few moments to tear the sheets into strips and to bind and gag the helpless man. Then Jack and Frank left the cabin.

At almost the same instant von Ludwig and Harris came from a second cabin.

"All right?" asked von Ludwig.

"All right, sir. And you?"

"Everything shipshape. Now for the crew. First, however," he said, addressing Jack and Frank, "don the clothing of these two officers. You shall be my second and third in command."

The lads returned to the cabin they had just quitted and stripped the prisoner. Jack donned the uniform, for the German was a big man. Then they hurried into the second cabin and performed a similar operation and Frank soon was attired in the uniform of a German lieutenant.

"Now," said von Ludwig, "have the crew report here and keep your guns ready."

Frank made his way aft, and in German, called:

"All hands forward!"

The crew came tumbling from their bunks and hurried forward, most of the men no more than half dressed. Jack, Frank and Harris, on either side of von Ludwig, confronted them.

"Men," said von Ludwig, "I am the new commander of this ship and we shall get under way immediately. Fearing that you will not always obey my commands, I have brought along these little persuaders."

A pair of automatics flashed in his hands and covered the ten sailors.

"Hands up!" he cried.

Taken completely by surprise there was nothing for the German sailors to do but obey. Up went their hands. Von Ludwig called to Harris.

"Help me keep them covered," he said, "while you other two tie them up."

Under the muzzles of the revolvers levelled in steady hands by von Ludwig and Harris, Jack and Frank set to work binding the members of the crew. A few minutes later the work was done.

"Trundle them into that cabin there," said von Ludwig, motioning to an open door. "Tie them there so they cannot release their own bonds or the bonds of the others. Then report to me on deck."

The lads obeyed. It was the work of only a few moments, struggle as the

Germans did. Then Frank and Jack went on deck.

A short distance away a rowboat was coming rapidly toward the Bismarck—for such was the name of the vessel on which the lads found themselves.

Von Ludwig pointed to it.

"My crew!" he said quietly.

CHAPTER XXVI

DISCOVERED

A few moments later the little skiff scraped alongside the Bismarck. One at a time its occupants—five in number—scrambled over the side and stood before von Ludwig. The latter scrutinized each man closely.

"All right," he said at length.

He selected three men.

"You report to the engine room immediately," he said. "You will find everything ready. The crew has been overpowered and there will be no one to interfere with you."

The men moved away. Von Ludwig addressed the other two.

"Take the lookout forward," he said to one; and to the other: "Go aft and keep your eyes open." Then he spoke to Harris. "I'll appoint you in command in the engine room," he said. "Heed your signals carefully."

Harris saluted.

"Very well, sir," he said and disappeared.

Von Ludwig motioned to Jack and Frank, who followed him to the bridge.

The officer cast a quick glance over the water and said:

"I guess there is no reason to delay longer. Mr. Chadwick, will you take the wheel? I'll be with you in a moment to give you your directions."

Frank moved away. Von Ludwig was just about to address Jack when he made out another rowboat coming toward the Bismarck.

"Hello!" he said aloud. "Wonder what's up now. Guess we'd better wait a minute."

The rowboat drew closer and Frank discovered it was filled with men.

"Boat crowded with men, sir," he exclaimed.

"So!" exclaimed von Ludwig. "Then I guess we won't wait, after all. You may get under way, Mr. Templeton."

With this order von Ludwig took his place beside Frank at the wheel and produced a chart. The bell in the engine room tinkled. A moment later the engines began to move and the Bismarck slipped easily through the water.

Came a hail from the rowboat.

"Wait a moment, there!"

Von Ludwig paid no attention to this call. The Bismarck gathered headway.

"Haven't time to talk to you fellows," said von Ludwig. "We want to be a long ways from here before daylight."

There was a sound of a shot from the rowboat, followed by many other shots. Von Ludwig waved a hand in derision.

"You're too late," he called. "Shoot away. I don't think you will hit anything."

"But, sir," said Frank, "they will awaken every sleepy German hereabouts."

"That's so," said von Ludwig. He called to Jack: "Full speed ahead, Mr.

Templeton."

Jack gave the word and the vessel dashed ahead.

"I don't know anything about these waters, sir," exclaimed Frank, in some alarm. "There may be mines about."

"Not here," was von Ludwig's reply. "Farther on, yes. That's why I have this chart. We'll run the mine fields safely enough, barring accidents."

"What is my course, sir?" asked Frank.

"Due north until I tell you to change."

Frank said nothing further, but guided the vessel according to instructions. Behind, the rowboat had given up the chase, but now, from other parts of the harbor, from which the Bismarck was fast speeding, came sounds of confusion.

Searchlights came to play upon the Bismarck.

Von Ludwig sighed deeply.

"I was in hopes we would get away without trouble," he said, "but it seems we won't. The erstwhile commander of this vessel must have discovered in some manner that he has been fooled."

"We'll have every ship of war hereabouts after us, sir," said Frank.

"That's what we will," was Von Ludwig's reply. "However, I am not afraid of their catching us. This vessel has the heels of anything in this port. Trouble is, though, they may tip off vessels on the outside of our coming, by wireless."

"What shall we do then, sir?"

"We'll have to manage to get by them some way; for if we should be caught now it would mean the noose for all of us."

"Not a very cheerful prospect, sir," said Frank, quietly.

"I agree with you. However, they haven't caught us yet. We'll give them a hard race."

"Is the vessel armed, sir?"

"It should be, if I have been informed correctly. I'll have a look about. Hold to your course until I return."

He moved away. He was back in a few moments, however, with the announcement that there were four 12-pounders aft, as well as four forward.

"Enough to fight with," he announced gravely.

"But we haven't the men to man them, sir," protested Frank.

"We'll impress our prisoners into service if it's necessary. With a man to guard them they can handle the engine room."

"I am afraid it will come to that, sir," said Frank.

Von Ludwig shrugged.

"What will be, will be," he replied quietly.

And it did come to that, as Frank had predicted As the vessel still flew through the water at full speed, there came a sudden cry from the lookout forward:

"Cruiser off our port bow, sir!"

Von Ludwig sprang forward. He gazed at the vessel quickly and then called to Frank:

"Port your helm hard!"

Frank obeyed without question and the Bismarck swung about sharply.

Von Ludwig sprang to his side.

"They'll pick us up with their searchlight in a minute or two," he cried. "Come with me, Templeton! Chadwick, hold that course till I come back."

Jack sprang after von Ludwig. The latter hurried to the cabin where the German prisoners were confined. He unloosened the bonds of five.

"You men," he said sharply, "will go before us to the engine room, where you will perform the necessary duties."

Under the muzzles of the weapons of Jack and von Ludwig, the men obeyed, for there seemed nothing else to do. In the engine room von Ludwig explained:

"I want you men to put forth your best efforts. Any foolishness and you will be shot, for I will take no chances. Harris, can you guard them?"

"Yes, sir," replied Harris, with a smile. "Give me another gun, sir."

Von Ludwig passed a revolver to Harris.

"There must be no half way methods here," he said quietly. "Shoot the first man who makes a false move. Ask questions afterward. Our lives depend upon it."

"I shall obey your instructions, sir."

"Good!" Von Ludwig addressed the former engine-room crew. "Follow me, men," he exclaimed.

No questions were asked and the others followed Jack and von Ludwig from the room, leaving Harris in command of the German crew of five. These Germans, under the muzzles of Harris' two revolvers, fell to work immediately.

Von Ludwig led the former engine-room crew to the guns forward.

"Man these guns," he said quietly. "There may be fighting to do. When I give the word fire as rapidly and as accurately as possible at the closest enemy vessel."

"Very well, sir," said one of the men.

Von Ludwig called to Jack to follow him and returned to the bridge. There he gave a slight alteration in course to Frank and the vessel's head turned slightly.

"Funny they haven't raised us with that searchlight," von Ludwig muttered to himself.

The Bismarck was dashing through the water at a rapid gait. Suddenly she became the center of a blinding glare. The searchlight of a German cruiser a half a mile to port had picked them up. Von Ludwig gave a sharp command to the men who manned the forward guns.

"Aim and fire!" he cried.

A moment later one of the guns spoke and a shell screamed across the water toward the German cruiser. Apparently it did not find its mark, however, for nothing happened aboard the enemy to indicate the shot had struck home.

"Again!" cried von Ludwig.

Another gun boomed. Followed a sharp explosion.

"Good work, men!" cried von Ludwig. "Try it again."

But the next shot came from the enemy. A shell screamed overhead.

"They'll do better with the next shot, sir," said Jack, quietly.

"So they will," was von Ludwig's quiet response. "Starboard your helm,

Mr. Chadwick."

Frank obeyed immediately, and again the course of the Bismarck was changed quickly; and none too soon.

For another salvo had come from the German cruiser and two shells flew past the spot where the Bismarck would have been at that moment had her course not suddenly been altered.

"Fire, men!" cried von Ludwig. "Fire as fast as you can. If you can't disable her we are done for!"

The men who manned the Bismarck's guns were working like Trojans. Once, twice, thrice more they fired; and upon the fourth shot there came a cry of dismay from aboard the enemy cruiser.

"Must have hit something, sir," said Frank.

"Right. I trust it was a vulnerable spot."

Twice more the German cruiser fired at the Bismarck, but without result. The smaller vessel was drawing ahead rapidly now.

"Fifteen minutes and we will be safe," said von Ludwig.

The men aboard the Bismarck continued to fire at the German cruiser, but apparently none of the other shots found their mark. The German, it could be seen, was in full pursuit, but the smaller vessel forged rapidly ahead with each turn of her screws. And at last von Ludwig exclaimed thankfully:

"Well, I guess we are safe enough here."

But even as he spoke a cry apprised him of a newer and closer danger!

CHAPTER XXVII

A TERRIBLE STRUGGLE

The trouble had started in the engine room. Hardly had the Bismarck drawn clear of the fire of the German cruiser when one of the five members of the German crew impressed into service fell over, apparently in a dead faint. The men, under Harris' watchful eye, had been working hard and the first thought that struck the Englishman was that the man had dropped from exhaustion.

Hastily he shoved one of his automatics in his belt and advancing, stooped over the man. Instantly, the other four Germans rushed for him.

Harris heard them coming and attempted to get to his feet. He was too late. A heavy shovel, wielded by one of his four assailants, struck him a hard blow over the head and Harris fell to the deck unconscious. Quickly the men relieved him of his two weapons and then they held a consultation.

"We must release the others first," said one man.

This plan was agreed upon and the man who had suggested it was appointed to make his way to where the others were imprisoned and free them. A moment later he slipped stealthily from the engine room and as stealthily approached the cabin where his fellow countrymen were imprisoned. Inside, he closed the door quickly and in a low voice cautioned the others to silence.

Quickly he unloosened their bonds and the five sailors and two officers rose and stretched their cramped limbs. In a few words the German sailor gave his officers the lay of the land and the first lieutenant took command.

"In the next cabin," he said, "is a chest containing revolvers and ammunition. Bring it here."

Two men hurried to obey and returned a few moments later bearing the chest. The two officers armed themselves and the men.

"These English must be very careless," said one, "else we would never have this chance."

The others agreed and the two officers considered what was best to be done.

"How many are there, did you say?" asked the first officer of the man who had released the others.

"There were nine, but we have disposed of the man in the engine room."

"Then we are twelve to eight. Good! First we will try and capture the bridge and the wheel. As we are in command of the engine room, the rest should be easy. It will not be necessary to capture all the English. With the bridge, wheel and engine room in our possession, we can run the vessel back into the harbor. Come on, men!"

They advanced quietly from the cabin and made their way on deck. It was the appearance of the first head that had called forth a cry from one of the British that had attracted von Ludwig's attention. Wheeling quickly, von Ludwig saw the Germans dash from below.

With a quick cry to the others, he drew his revolver and fired. One man toppled over. The odds against the British were one less; but the others sprang forward. Frank, at the wheel, was forced to maintain his position while the others did the fighting.

The lookout forward and the man stationed aft advanced to take part in the fray, though keeping out of sight as well as possible.

"Turn the gun on them, men!" cried von Ludwig.

The three men who manned the gun sought to obey, but the gun stuck. It would not turn. Most likely it had been damaged in the battle with the German cruiser. The British tried the other guns, but with no better result.

"Stay where you are," shouted van Ludwig to the men at the guns. "Keep them between us, if possible."

The gun crew, who had been on the point of trying to join von Ludwig and Jack, saw the strategy of this plan and stooped down behind the guns. The lookout forward also stepped behind the mainmast, where he began to blaze away at the foe. The man aft, by a dash, succeeded in reaching the side of von Ludwig and Jack.

Frank, at the wheel, was in a perilous situation, but there he had determined to stay until ordered to shift his position.

"Signal the engine room to slow down," said von Ludwig to Jack.

Jack obeyed and the ship came to a pause. Apparently the men below believed the Germans had recaptured the ship.

"If Harris is still in command down there, we are all right," said von Ludwig. "If not, there will be more of the enemy up here in a minute."

And within a minute more of the enemy appeared.

"Back here, Chadwick!" exclaimed von Ludwig. "Never mind the wheel."

Frank sprang to the shelter of the bridge, Jack and von Ludwig protecting his retreat. Frank drew his revolver.

A German poked his head from the companion-way and Frank took a snap shot. The head disappeared and there was a howl of pain.

"Got one, I guess," said the lad quietly.

The effect of this shot was to infuriate the Germans. The first officer commanded a charge on the bridge.

Ten men dashed forward at the word.

Now the four in the shelter of the bridge—von Ludwig, Frank, Jack and the man who had come from the after part of the vessel, stood to their full height and fired into the crowd. From the rear, the three other British also poured in a volley and the lookout stepped into the open and fired.

Caught thus between three fires, the Germans were at a loss what to do.

One man dropped and the others dashed for the protection of the companionway. Before reaching there, however, the first German officer gave the command to scatter and several of the Germans posted themselves behind whatever shelter offered on deck. The battle had reached a deadlock.

The British could not expose themselves without danger of being struck by a German bullet; and the Germans confronted the same situation.

"Signal the engine room, Jack," instructed von Ludwig. "We must know whether Harris is still alive."

There was no response to the signal.

"Poor fellow," said von Ludwig. "They probably have done for him."

From time to time Jack signalled the engine room, thinking perhaps that Harris had only been wounded and that he might answer. Upon the fifth signal he received an answer.

Then Jack signalled: "Full speed ahead."

A moment later the vessel leaped forward. There came a cry of consternation from the Germans, who tumbled back down the steps. As they did so, Frank again sprang to the wheel and brought the head of the Bismarck sharply about—for since he had released his hold on the wheel the vessel had been drifting.

Quickly the lad lashed the wheel with several lengths of cable and then sprang back to the bridge amid a volley of revolver bullets from the Germans who still held the deck. None hit him.

Below, in the engine room, Harris was facing heavy odds. Before answering Jack's signal, after regaining consciousness, he had closed and barred the engine-room door and now he paid no attention to the hammering upon it. He smiled grimly to himself.

"You won't get in here as long as that door holds," he said. "Before that I should have assistance."

The pounding upon the door continued.

"We'll have to lend Harris a hand, sir," said Jack. "They are too many for him down there."

"The first man that steps clear of this bridge is likely to get shot," declared von Ludwig. "However, as you say, we must lend him a hand." He called to the men who were still safe behind the guns. "Make a rush this way," he said. "We'll cover your retreat."

A moment later three forms flitted across the deck. Two German heads were raised from their cover. Frank accounted for one and von Ludwig for the other. Thus were three of the enemy placed hors de combat. Seven had rushed below. There were still two left on deck.

A spurt of flame showed Jack where one was hidden.

With a quick move the lad sprang from the bridge and threw himself to the deck on his face. There was another spurt of flame and a bullet whistled over his head. Before the man could fire again, Jack had leaped forward and seized him by his revolver arm. Angrily, the lad wrested the weapon from the man's grasp.

The latter drew a knife. There was but one thing for Jack to do. Quickly he raised his revolver, pointed it squarely at the German's face, and fired.

A flash of flame had betrayed the hiding place of the last German on deck. Two of the British rushed for him. The German accounted for both of them before they could reach him.

The losses so far, had been two British and four of the enemy. There were still six British on deck and a single German; but seven Teutons were still hammering at the door of the engine room in an effort to get at Harris.

"We've got to get rid of this fellow on deck," muttered Frank. He spoke to one of the men near him.

"You advance from one side and I'll advance from the other," said the lad quietly. "The man, apparently, is a dead shot and he probably will get one of us. But he's dangerous there. He may fire at you and he may fire at me, but the other will get him."

The man nodded that he understood, and one from each side of the bridge they advanced.

As it transpired it was not Frank who was to pay the penalty for this

rash advance. Perceiving two men approaching, one from either side, the

German fired. Quickly, Frank raised his revolver and also fired. The

German threw up his arms and fell to the deck.

Frank turned quickly and looked for the man who had left the shelter of the bridge with him. He lay prone on the deck.

"Poor fellow," said Frank. "Yet it had to be done. Just luck that it wasn't me."

"Deck's clear, sir," said Frank to von Ludwig. "Now to lend Harris a hand in the engine room."

"Forward, then," said von Ludwig. "All except you, Frank, and you, Jack. You two stay on deck. Take the wheel again, Frank. Jack, you stand at the head of the companionway and shoot the first German who appears there."

"Very well, sir," said Jack, although he was disappointed that he was not permitted to go to Harris' aid.

"The others follow me," said von Ludwig.

There were but two other men that could follow.

"You are attempting too much, sir," said Jack.

"I think not," said von Ludwig, calmly.

He led the way below.

CHAPTER XXVIII

THE CHEATING OF HARRIS

Below, Harris had just armed himself with a great iron bar; for he knew that the door was about to give under the attacks of the Germans.

"The fools!" he said to himself. "Why don't they blow the lock off?"

It seemed that the same thought struck the German first officer at about the same moment. Motioning his men back, he approached the door and put the muzzle of his revolver against the lock. He pulled the trigger, and when the Germans again surged against the door it flew open beneath their weight.

One man stumbled headlong through the door. As he did so, Harris raised his heavy bar and brought it down on the man's head. The German dropped with a crushed skull.

But before Harris could raise his weapon again the Germans had closed about him and sought to strike him down with the butts of their revolvers. The struggling figures were so closely entwined now that the enemy could not fire without fear of hitting one of their own number.

Harris struck out right and left and men staggered back before his terrific blows. Then came the sounds of running footsteps without.

"Back!" called the German first officer.

Two British heads appeared in the doorway almost simultaneously.

"Crack! Crack! Crack! Crack!"

The Germans poured a volley into the two men and the latter sagged to the deck.

Harris, at the same moment, had jumped toward the door. As he leaped over the prostrate forms, he collided with von Ludwig.

"Quick, sir!" he cried. "They are too many for us. Back on deck!"

There was something in Harris' manner that impressed von Ludwig. Without stopping to argue, he followed Harris. When both were safe on deck, Harris quickly closed the door of the companionway and battened it down.

"We've a breathing spell, at any rate," he said, mopping his face.

"Why all this rush?" demanded von Ludwig. "Where are the men who went to your assistance?"

"Dead, the same as we would be if we had lingered another moment," replied Harris, quietly. "It was impossible to pass through that door without being shot down. It was only due to the diversion of the appearance of the others that permitted me to escape."

Came heavy blows against the covering of the companionway.

"They want to come out," said Harris, grinning.

"That door won't stand much battering," said von Ludwig.

"No, it won't," was Harris' reply, "but one man can guard it well enough. Besides, we have the bridge. We can steer the vessel where we will."

"As long as the engines run we can," agreed von Ludwig. "But unless I'm greatly mistaken the Germans will soon stop them."

He was right; for a few moments later the battering at the door of the companionway ceased and the engines ceased work.

"Well, we can't go any place now, sir," said Frank, leaving the wheel and approaching von Ludwig and Harris at the companionway.

Jack also came up to them.

"You're right," agreed von Ludwig, "and that's not the worst of it. The German cruiser probably is in pursuit of us. If they sight us we are done for."

Came more violent blows on the door over the companionway, followed by a shot from below.

Jack sprang aside as a bullet plowed its way through the hard wood.

"We'll have to stand to one side," he said. "Otherwise, they are likely to drop one of us."

"The door will stand considerable battering," said von Ludwig. "There is but one thing I can think of. We shall have to desert the ship."

"In what, a rowboat?" asked Frank, with some sarcasm.

"Hardly," returned von Ludwig; "but I have discovered that there is a high-powered motor boat aboard. We can launch that and move off."

"And as soon as the Germans break out here, they'll come after us and shoot us full of holes," said Harris.

"Well, that's true enough, too," agreed von Ludwig. "Of course, if we had an hour's start we might get through. But the door won't hold that long."

Harris had been turning a plan over in his mind.

"If you please, sir," he said slowly at last, "I have a plan that may work."

"Let's hear it," said Frank.

"Yes; let's have it," said von Ludwig.

"Well," said Harris, "one man, with a couple of revolvers, should be able to guard this passageway for an hour without trouble. He can shoot the Germans down as fast as they come up. My plan is this. Let one man stay behind on guard. The others can put off in the motor boat."

"But the one man will die," said Frank.

"Of course," said Harris, simply. "That shall be my job."

"Not much," said Jack. "I'll pick that job for myself."

"Not while I'm here you won't," declared Frank. "I'm plenty big to guard the companionway."

"The plan you suggest, Harris," von Ludwig said quietly, "is the only one, so far as I can see, that promises any degree of success. In my pocket are papers that must reach the British admiralty at the earliest possible moment."

"Then there is no reason why you should think of staying, sir," said

Harris.

"Wait," said von Ludwig. "In a venture such as this, there is no reason one man should be called upon to sacrifice himself more than another. We shall all have an even chance."

"What do you mean, sir?" asked Frank.

"Simply this. We shall draw lots to see who shall remain."

"Suits me," said Harris, with a shrug.

"And me," declared Jack.

"Well, then I'm agreeable," Frank said quietly.

"Good. Harris, in the pocket of my coat, which hangs in the pilot house, you will find a pack of cards. Bring them here."

Harris walked away and returned a few seconds later with a pack of playing cards. Von Ludwig opened the box and produced the cards.

"The man who cuts the lowest card shall stay behind," he said quietly.

"Shuffle."

He passed the cards to Harris, who riffled them lightly.

"One moment," said von Ludwig. "If I should be the man to stay, I want one of you to take these papers in my pocket. They must be turned over to the admiralty at the earliest possible moment. Should the man who carries them be in danger of capture, they must be destroyed. Do you understand?"

"Yes, sir," said Jack.

Frank nodded.

"It shall be as you say, sir," said Harris, "Now who will cut first?"

"It may as well be me as another," said von Ludwig.

He cut the cards and exposed to view a jack of hearts.

"Looks like you will carry the papers yourself, sir," said Frank, as he advanced to cut the cards.

He held up a nine spot of spades.

"That lets you out, sir," he said to von Ludwig.

The latter was plainly nervous.

Jack cut the cards next. Frank uttered a cry of consternation:

"The three of clubs!"

"Looks like I was the fellow to stay, all right," said Jack, smiling slightly.

"And this time," said Frank, "you may not be as fortunate as upon the day you remained behind and faced death on the submarine."

Jack shrugged.

"Can't be helped," he said quietly.

Now Harris advanced and cut the cards quickly.

As he picked up the upper half of the deck, he turned his shoulder slightly so that the others, for the moment, might not see what he had cut. He glanced at the bottom card. It was the six of diamonds.

Deftly, Harris shuffled the cards with his hands. Adept in the art of trickery, though the others did not know it, he had placed the cards in such position that he knew almost identically where the high and low cards were.

Like a flash his hand passed across the bottom of the deck and when it was withdrawn the six of diamonds had disappeared. Then he turned to the others and exposed:

The two spot of spades!

"I lose," he said quietly.

Harris' movements had been so quick that they had not been perceived by the others.

Jack was the first to extend a hand.

"I'm sorry," the lad said quietly. "I was in hopes that it would be me."

As he shook hands with the others, Harris kept his left hand behind him; for in it reposed the card he had palmed—the six of diamonds, which would have allowed him to go with the others and would have put Jack in his place.

As he turned, Harris slipped the card quickly into his pocket, that it might not be accidentally seen. Then, he knew, he was safe.

Jack picked up the deck.

"I shall keep these, Harris," he said, "that I may always remember a brave man."

All this time the thundering on the door of the companionway had continued.

"Come," said von Ludwig, "we must delay no longer. Already it is growing light."

He hastened along the deck to where the high-powered motor boat lay covered with a tarpaulin. Quickly the little craft was lowered over the side, von Ludwig first inspecting it.

"Plenty of water and provisions," he said quietly. He turned to Harris.

"It is time to say goodbye," he said quietly. "You are a brave man.

This gallant action shall be known to the world."

"Goodbye, sir," said Harris, quietly.

"Remember," said von Ludwig, "there is always a chance that you may escape. If it comes, make the most of it. Goodbye."

He pressed Harris' hand and passed over the side of the vessel.

As Frank and Jack shook hands with Harris, the latter squeezed Harris' hand affectionately. The latter smiled.

"I had promised myself another bout with you some day," he said. "My only regret is that it is not possible now."

A moment more Jack was in the motor boat and it moved away. Harris drew his revolvers and mounted guard over the companionway, the door of which now had begun to splinter.

"An hour is what you needed," he said quietly. "You'll get it!"

CHAPTER XXIX

A CHAMPION PASSES

Harris laid one of his revolvers on the deck, reached in his pocket and produced the six of diamonds. He looked at it closely in the half darkness and a smile passed over his face.

"I suppose I'm a fool," he muttered to himself, "but someway I couldn't help it. I was afraid Jack would cut the low card. I wouldn't have done it for one of the others, but Jack, well, he's a boy after my own heart."

Harris replaced the card in his pocket; then thought better of his action, drew it forth again and sent it spinning off across the sea.

"There," he said quietly, "goes all evidence that I cheated."

He picked up the revolver he had laid on the deck and moved a short distance from the companionway.

There was an extra violent crash and it seemed that the door must burst open.

"Another one like that will do the work," said Harris, calmly.

He took up what he considered a strategic position and produced his watch. This he lay on the deck and sat down beside it.

"May as well be comfortable," he remarked.

Again there was a crash and the door of the companionway burst open. A German head appeared.

"Crack!" Harris had fired without moving from his sitting posture.

The German head disappeared and there was a cry of alarm from below.

"One down, I guess," said Harris, quietly, to himself.

For some moments there was silence, broken occasionally, however, by the dull sound of voices from below.

"Talking it over, eh?" muttered Harris. "Well, I'll still be here when you try again."

It was perhaps fifteen minutes later that a cap appeared in the opening. Again Harris fired. The cap did not disappear and Harris fired twice more quickly.

The cap disappeared.

"Guess I got another one," said Harris.

Twice more within the next fifteen minutes this happened.

"That should be four, if I have counted correctly," said Harris; "and

I've still four cartridges left. I won't have to reload yet."

He felt in his pocket and then uttered an exclamation of alarm.

"No more bullets. I'll have to make these four count for the next two."

Nothing appeared in the doorway again for ten minutes more and then

Harris fired again. Fifteen minutes later the same thing happened and

Harris, making sure that this was the last of the enemy, emptied his

revolver at it.

Then he got to his feet and put his watch in his pocket.

"Guess that settles it," he said. "Now I'll look around for a boat. I didn't know it was going to be as easy as all that. If I had I would have had the others wait for me."

He moved toward the companionway, and as he did so, a bullet whistled by his ear. Harris stepped back in surprise; and in that moment the solution came to him.

"By Jove! They've fooled me," he muttered. "They poked their caps up and I shot them full of holes. However, they don't know yet that I'm out of bullets."

A few moments later a cap again appeared in the opening. Harris had no bullets to fire at it.

"They'll discover my predicament in a moment or so, though," he told himself.

He pulled his watch from his pocket and glanced at it.

"An hour," he said. "They have had time enough. However, I'll just see the thing through."

As he spoke it grew light. Harris looked off across the sea. There, so far away that it appeared but a speck upon the water, he saw what he took to be the motor boat bearing his friends to safety. He waved his cap.

"Good luck!" he said quietly.

Now a German head appeared in the door of the companionway. It was not a cap this time. Harris saw it, and drawing back his arm, hurled one of his revolvers swiftly. His aim was true and the weapon struck the German squarely in the face. With a scream of pain the man fell back into the arms of his companions.

But Harris' action had told his enemies that he had no more bullets, and seeing that they had but one man to contend with, the Germans sprang from their shelter and leaped for him.

Harris clubbed his remaining revolver, and with his back to the pilot house, where he had retreated, awaited the approach of the four foes.

"You're going to have the fight of your lives," he said grimly.

A German sprang. Harris' arm rose and fell and there was one German less to contend with. But before Harris could raise his arm again, the other three had closed in upon him. Harris felt himself borne back.

The former pugilistic champion of the British navy cast all ring ethics to the winds. He struck, kicked and clawed and sought to wreak what damage he could upon his enemies without regard for the niceties of fighting. He knew that they would do the same to him.

So great had been the force of the shock of the three Germans—all that were now left of the original twelve—that Harris was borne to the deck. His revolver hand struck the floor with great force and the weapon was sent spinning from his grasp.

With a mighty effort, he hurled the three men from him and leaped to his feet. The Germans also arose. Harris did not wait for them to resume the offensive. With head lowered he charged.

Nimbly the foe skipped to either side and Harris felt a keen pain in his right side. One of the foe had drawn a knife and stabbed as Harris rushed by. Whirling quickly, Harris again sprang forward. One man did not leap out of his way quickly enough, and Harris' hands found his throat.

The man gave a screech as Harris' hands squeezed. The Englishman raised his enemy bodily from the deck, flung him squarely in the faces of the other two, and followed after the human catapult.

The foremost German dodged and seized Harris by the legs. Both went over in a heap, Harris on top. Harris raised his right fist and would have brought it down on the German's face but for the fact that the second foe seized his arm in a fierce grasp. At the same moment he struck with his knife.

The point penetrated Harris' right side and he felt himself growing faint. Angrily, he shook the German from him and rose to his feet. The man who had been underneath the Englishman also got quickly to his feet, and before Harris could turn, stabbed him in the back.

With a cry, Harris whirled on him and seized the knife arm. He twisted sharply. The German cried out in pain and sought to free himself. But his effort was in vain.

With the grasp by the wrist, Harris swung the man in the air, and spinning on his heel, hurled him far across the deck, where the unconscious form struck with a crash; and at the same moment the other German struck again with his knife.

Harris staggered back.

Now the German who so recently had felt the effect of Harris' fingers in his throat, pulled himself from the deck and renewed the battle. He advanced, crouching, and another knife gleamed in his hand.

It is possible that, had it not been for the effects of the knife wounds, Harris, in the end, would have overcome these foes, for he was a powerful man. But when a man is bleeding from half a dozen wounds and faces two adversaries both armed with knives, he has little chance of ultimate victory. Harris realized it; but he was not the man to beg for mercy. Besides, so fierce had been his attacks and so great his execution, it is not probable that the Germans would have spared him anyhow. They were insane with rage.

There were only two of them left now; and Harris told himself that their number would be fewer by one before they finished with him. He leaned against the pilot house panting from his exertions.

"A great lot of fighters, you are," he taunted his enemies. "Four of you attacked me with knives and you haven't done for me yet."

The Germans also were glad of a breathing spell. Their faces reddened as Harris taunted them.

"We shall kill you yet," said one angrily.

"Don't be too sure," said Harris. "I'm an Englishman, you know, and you have always been afraid of an Englishman."

At this the Germans uttered a cry of rage and sprang forward, their knives flashing aloft.

The first German missed his mark as Harris dodged beneath his arm and closed with him. He uttered a cry for help.

"That's right, you coward! You'll need it," said Harris.

He squeezed the man with all his might. Out of the tail of his eye he caught the glint of the other German's knife as it descended. Releasing his hold upon the one man, he stepped quickly backward. But the knife caught him a glancing blow on the forehead, inflicting a deep wound.

For a moment Harris paused to shake the blood out of his eyes. Then, with a smile playing across his features, he advanced; and as he advanced he said:

"You've done for me, the lot of you. But I shall take you with me."

The Germans quailed at the look in his face; and as he moved forward swiftly they threw down their knives and turned to run.

But they had delayed too long.

Harris stretched both hands out straight before him. One hand closed about the arm of the German to his right. The other clutched the second man by the throat. Harris pulled the man he held by the arm close; then released his grip, but before the German could stagger away, seized him, too, by the throat.

"Now I've got you," he said.

Blow after blow the Germans rained upon his face and shoulders, kicking out with their feet the while. Harris paid no more attention to these than he would have to the taps of a child.

But the Englishman felt his strength waning fast. It was with an effort that he staggered across the deck. At the rail he paused for a moment, gathering his strength for a final effort.

Then, still holding a German by the throat with each hand, he leaped into the sea.

Once, twice, three times the three heads appeared on the surface and a spectator could have seen that Harris retained his grip. Then the three sank from sight.

And so passed the former pugilistic champion of the British fleet, brave in death as he had been in life. The waves washed over the spot where he had gone down.

CHAPTER XXX

THE UNKNOWN UNMASKS

With the coming of dawn the three figures in the little motor boat gazed back in the direction from whence they had come. There they could still make out the distant shape of the Bismarck. She rode quietly in the water, and there was nothing about her appearance to tell the three in the motor boat of the terrible struggle that was raging even at that moment.

"Poor Harris," said Jack. "I hope that in some manner he is able to escape."

"Certainly I hope so, too," declared Frank.

"He's a brave man," said von Ludwig.

Jack drew the fateful deck of cards from his pocket.

"These," he said, "I shall keep."

He ran through the deck several times, playing with them. Unconsciously he counted them.

There was something wrong. Jack counted the cards again. The result was the same.

"Sir!" he called to von Ludwig.

"Well?" "How did you chance to have this pack of cards?"

"I play solitaire considerably," was the reply.

"You couldn't have played solitaire with this deck," said Jack.

"Why not?"

"All the cards are not here. There are but fifty-one."

"There were fifty-two when I put them in my pocket," said von Ludwig, "because I counted them."

Again Jack ran through the deck There were but fifty-one cards. Suddenly the lad gave a start. He spread the cards out in the bottom of the boat, making four piles all suits together. He counted the hearts. They were all there, thirteen of them. He counted the clubs. They were all there, too. Next he counted the spades. All were there. Last he counted the diamonds. There were but twelve. Jack arranged them in order. There was one card shy. Jack found what it was a moment later. There was no six of diamonds in the deck. For some moments Jack sat silent, staring at the cards before him. He had been struck with a great light.

"So!" he said to himself at last, "Harris cheated."

"What's that?" said Frank, who had heard Jack's muttered words, but had not caught their import.

"I said," replied Jack, slowly, "that Harris cheated."

Frank was surprised. A moment later he said: "Well, even if he did, he lost anyhow."

"That's it," said Jack, quietly. "He didn't lose."

"You mean——" exclaimed Frank, excitedly.

"Yes; I mean that I lost. I should have been the one to stay."

"Impossible," said Frank.

"It's true," declared Jack. "Von Ludwig here says the deck was a full deck. It's shy a card now. The six of diamonds is missing. That is the card Harris cut first. You remember he turned aside?"

"Yes, but——"

"That's when he slipped the six of diamonds out of sight and exposed the deuce of spades."

"What's all this talk about cards?" asked von Ludwig, at this juncture.

Jack explained and for a few moments von Ludwig was lost in thought.

"You know," he said, finally, "I think more of that fellow every minute.

That's the one case I have ever heard of where a man cheated with honor."

There was silence aboard the little craft as it sped over the water, all three aboard keeping a close watch for the approach of a German vessel of some sort. Von Ludwig referred to his chart occasionally, for he wished to steer as clear of mines as possible. They might be deep in the water and they might be close to the surface. There was no use taking chances. And while the voyage continued the lads were to be treated to yet another surprise; but this surprise was to be a pleasure and would not bring heavy hearts, as had the discovery of the missing card.

"I wish," said Jack, suddenly, to von Ludwig, "that you would tell me who you really are. I sit here and look at you and know I should be able to call your name. But I can't do it and it makes it decidedly unpleasant."

Von Ludwig smiled. "I should have thought you would know me in a minute in spite of my disguise," he said quietly. "I am sure I should have known both of you no matter what pains you took to conceal your features."

"You're only making matters worse," said Frank. "Come on now and tell us who you are."

Again von Ludwig smiled. "I wonder if you can guess who I am when I say

that I can tell you all about yourselves?" he said. "For instance, you,

Jack. You spent most of your life in a little African village. And you,

Frank, are an American who was shanghaied aboard a sailing vessel in

Naples soon after the outbreak of the war."

"By Jove!" said Jack. "Outside of Frank here there is only one man who knows all that about me."

"And there is but a single man who knows as much of me," declared Frank.

"Can it be——"

For answer von Ludwig rose in his seat and stripped from his face the heavy German beard that had given him the true Teutonic expression, and there stood revealed before Jack and Frank none other than Lord Hastings, their erstwhile commander and good friend. Frank gave a cry of delight and sprang forward at the imminent risk of upsetting the motor boat. He seized Lord Hastings' hand and pressed it warmly. The latter's greeting was no less affectionate. Jack, not so given to demonstrations as his chum, also advanced and grasped Lord Hasting's hand.

"You don't know how glad I am to see you again, sir," the lad said quietly. "It seems like an age since we saw you. And to think that we didn't recognize you instantly."

"That's what seemed so funny to me," said Lord Hastings. "When I first saw you aboard that German vessel I was fearful for a minute that you would recognize me and blurt it out right there."

"But what were you doing there, Lord Hastings?" asked Frank.

"It's a long story," was the latter's reply, "but I guess now is as good a time as any to explain."

"I wish you would, sir," said Jack.

"Well," said Lord Hastings, "as you know, I told you when we parted that I had an important diplomatic duty to perform. First, it carried me to Roumania, where, I may say, I was successful."

"You mean that Roumania has decided to cast in her fortunes with the

Allies, sir?"

"Exactly. She will take that step some time in August, though the exact date I am unable to say. My mission there at an end, I was ordered to report to Berlin. As you know, we still maintain a staff of correspondents in the German capital, although their identities are closely hidden."

Frank and Jack nodded, for they had known this some time before.

"Well," Lord Hastings continued, "in Berlin I was instructed to learn what Germany planned to do to offset the Roumanian menace, for she is sure to know of Roumanians decision by this time. I had some trouble, but I succeeded at last."

"And what will she do, sir?" asked Frank.

"That," was the reply, "I am unable to state at this minute. It is a secret that I am guarding carefully and I cannot even tell you lads about it."

Frank and Jack asked no further questions along that line.

"But how came you aboard the German vessel, sir?" Jack wanted to know.

Lord Hastings smiled.

"In Berlin," he said, "I was supposed to be a Roumanian officer, who had hopes of changing the attitude of that country. The Kaiser wished to show me how foolish it would be for the little Balkan state to join the Allies, and for that reason, had me shown through the German naval fortifications. That information, too, I am carrying back with me."

"But why didn't you tell us who you were in Bremen, sir?"

"I don't know. At first I guess because I wanted to surprise you both when you did learn who I was."

"But you told us not to try and learn who you were."

"Well, that was for a good reason. For, if you should have sought to pry, it might have aroused suspicions and there is no telling what would have happened."

"I see, sir," said Frank. "But you almost lost us when you didn't get back in time."

"I know that now. I wouldn't do the same thing again."

"And what are you going to do after you return to London, sir?" Frank wanted to know.

Again Lord Hastings smiled.

"That's hard to tell," he replied. "Still, I imagine it will not be very long before I feel a deck under my heels again."

"You mean you will leave the diplomatic service again, sir?" asked

Jack.

"I expect to. The king promised me a new command before he despatched me to the Balkans. But I do not know how long I shall be kept waiting."

"And when you get it, sir, will we go back with you?" asked Frank.

"Why," was the reply, "I should have thought that by this time you would perhaps have changed your minds."

"Never, sir," declared Jack, positively. "We would rather serve under you, sir."

"I'll see what can be done," Lord Hastings promised.

And with that the lads were forced to be content. Still, they knew well enough that Lord Hastings would do what he could to have them with him again.

"The main thing now," said Lord Hastings, "is to dodge the enemy and get back to England."

"With you here, sir," said Frank, "I am sure we shall get back safely."

And Frank proved a good prophet.

All that day they made their way slowly through the North Sea. Several times enemy ships were sighted, but, because the little motor boat lay so low in the water, the Germans did not see them.

With the coming of night, however, Lord Hastings increased the speed of the little craft. He felt that they were now beyond the German mine fields and that if another vessel were encountered it probably would be British.

And this proved to be the case.

Along toward morning of the second day, a British cruiser bore down on them. Soon all were aboard the vessel, which, when Lord Hastings informed the commander of the nature of the papers he carried, turned about and headed for London.

A day or two later, Frank and Jack again found themselves installed in the comfortable home of Lord Hastings, where they sat down to await what time might bring forth—confident, however, that it would not be long before they were upon active service under the command of their good friend, Lord Hastings.